The Cowboy's Second Chance Family

Cowboys of Whistle Rock Ranch, Book Three

Contemporary Western Romance

SHIRLEEN DAVIES

Books Series by Shirleen Davies

Historical Western Romances

Redemption Mountain
MacLarens of Fire Mountain Historical
MacLarens of Boundary Mountain

Romantic Suspense

Eternal Brethren Military Romantic Suspense
Peregrine Bay Romantic Suspense

Contemporary Western Romance

Cowboys of Whistle Rock Ranch
MacLarens of Fire Mountain Contemporary
Macklins of Whiskey Bend

The best way to stay in touch is to subscribe to my newsletter. Go to my Website ***www.shirleendavies.com*** and fill in your email and name in the
Join My Newsletter boxes. That's it!

Avalanche Ranch Press, LLC
PO Box 12618
Prescott, AZ 86304

Book design and conversions by Joseph Murray at 3rdplanetpublishing.com

Cover design by Sweet 'n Spicy Designs

ISBN: 978-1-947680-76-0

I care about quality, so if you find something in error,
please contact me via email at
shirleen@shirleendavies.com

Description

This cowboy will do everything possible to get his family back.
He never expected to uncover the treachery which tore his marriage apart.

Trace Griffin loved his life as a rodeo competitor. Leaving it behind to recover his family hadn't been a difficult choice. Blindsided years earlier when his wife wrongly accused him of cheating, he found a new focus. Accepting a job at a dude ranch brought him closer to her and their son, setting him on a course for discovering the truth.

Emma Griffin had never been able to purge her ex-husband from her thoughts...or her heart. Working as an assistant cook at a dude ranch provided independence for her and her son.

Learning Trace had been hired at the same ranch set off all her protective instincts. Vowing never to succumb again to the charismatic cowboy, she agreed to work with him to discover the truth behind the allegations which led to their divorce.

Neither were prepared for the firestorm they uncovered. Nor did they suspect the people behind the lies, payoffs, and stolen money.

Will learning the truth herald a new beginning for Emma and Trace?

The Cowboy's Second Chance Family, book three in the Cowboys of Whistle Rock Ranch Contemporary Western Romance series, is a clean and wholesome, full-length novel with an HEA.

The Cowboy's Second Chance Family

Chapter One

Brilliance, Wyoming
July

Rolling out of bed in the cheapest motel he could find on a side street in Brilliance, Wyoming, Trace Griffin looked at the change on the shabby bedside table, all he had left of his meager weekly finances.

Seven dollars and forty-three cents. Maybe enough for a cup of coffee and bagel at the bakery. He snorted at the thought. At today's prices, black coffee and toast would be closer to reality.

Last night marked his last visit to the Kick 'em Up Motel. The name fit. From what he could tell, the place rented a few rooms by the hour, as well as the night. His room could easily be one of them. Lumpy mattress, bedspread he'd bet hadn't been washed in years, and towels smelling stale and moldy. The manager would say they were environmentally friendly by not washing towels and sheets after each patron. He grimaced as he brushed his teeth, ignoring the plastic cups nearby, wondering what the health department would say.

Using the shower, he pumped up the hot water until it turned lukewarm and washed. At least the hand towel didn't smell. Trace used it to dry his hair and body.

Dressing, he checked the time. Five-thirty. Plenty of time for a quick breakfast and still arrive at the ranch before his seven o'clock appointment with Virgil Redman, one of the foremen at Whistle Rock Ranch.

Trace needed the job at this particular ranch for reasons Virgil didn't know. When the foreman found out, all Trace could do was beg forgiveness and hope his reasons didn't cost him the job.

Stuffing everything he owned into an old, battered duffel, he took a last look around, hoping he never had to stay in a place like this again. Maybe this move to Whistle Rock would be what changed his life.

Shoving the money into a pocket, he headed outside to his truck, throwing the duffel into the back seat. Trace had a good deal of money saved up, allowing himself a small withdrawal each week.

Until the last year, he'd been a professional rodeo star. Saddle broncs and bareback riding were his two events, earning him hundreds of thousands over his career. That had been before his career ending injury earlier in the year.

Now healed, his body was good enough to handle ranch work, even break the occasional wild horse when asked. It would betray him if he ever tried to compete at a professional level. Three doctors and the same conclusion. Quit the rodeo or spend the rest of his life in a wheelchair.

His plans required him to be a ranch hand who was able to walk and ride. Plus, there was a much more personal reason for going after the combination dude ranch foreman and cowboy job.

Trace's money stretched to a cup of coffee with free refills and a large Danish, more than he'd expected. Sitting at a coveted window at the front of Brilliance Coffee & Bakery, he watched as the line began to stretch outside. He'd arrived just in time.

Doing this in some towns could prove a problem. Those with large rodeos posed the biggest threat, as people sought out the big winners from the previous years. He expected no issue in Brilliance.

Climbing into his truck, Trace placed the to-go cup of coffee in the holder, and turned around toward the ranch. He'd arrive early, which was his intent. Being early every day couldn't hurt. Same with working late. It was what he'd done his entire life. Great for his profession, not so wonderful for his personal life.

Parking next to a row of trucks, jeeps, SUVs, and a few cars, he sat for a while, sipping coffee while staring toward the back of the large ranch lodge. The kitchen, rooms for the house staff, and room for guests upstairs, along with two large pantries and two freezers. He'd learned all this from talking to a couple of the ranch hands while waiting for the job interviews with Wyatt and Virgil. Ranch hands knew everything about what went on. The key was getting them to talk.

A knock on his window almost caused him to drop the coffee. Virgil stood outside, motioning for Trace to join him.

"Morning. You're a little early."

"Is that a problem, Virgil?"

"Not at all. The fact is, your work day will start right after breakfast, which Nacho brings over from the kitchen about six. We'll head for the bunkhouse so you can put your stuff away. Did you have breakfast this morning?"

"Coffee and a Danish."

"Not enough." Virgil opened the door to the bunkhouse and motioned him inside. "I set some food aside for you in the bunkhouse kitchen. Not much, but more than what you had."

Less than fifteen minutes later, they continued outside. Virgil introduced him around, explaining his duties while answering Trace's questions. Never did they walk close to the house, for which he was grateful. There'd be time. He had nothing except time.

"I know you can work with horses. The most important task now is to get you acclimated to everything about the dude ranch. It's been in operation for a few weeks. We still have eight weeks to go. Our goal is to expand a little next year, though the weather will control much of what we do."

"When do guests arrive and leave?"

"Sundays. Some continue for a second week, most stay just one. The cabins sleep four. If a family comes in with three kids, we have rollaway beds. We don't allow anyone seven or younger. The ranch isn't designed for younger kids. Eight-year-olds are eager to get on a horse, and have the confidence to stay on during a two-hour trail ride. One hour out, stop for a break, and an hour back. We do offer longer rides. Those are for twelve and older."

Virgil continued toward the cabins. "We have twelve, with room for more if we get the demand." Reaching into a pocket, he pulled out a key card. "This is a master card. There are three more, plus individual key cards for each cabin. Wyatt and I have masters. You'll get one. That leaves one locked in Wyatt's office."

Opening the door, Virgil stepped inside. "Come on in." Showing Trace around, answering questions, including identifying the location of the water shut-off and electrical boxes. They stayed less than twenty minutes. "Any more questions?"

"Not right now. Where are the guests?"

"Everyone is on a morning hay ride. Wyatt is leading it, plus Barrel and a couple other ranch hands are riding along. Some of the guests are on horses while the rest are in two wagons. They took off right before you arrived. Breakfast is served on a trail near a waterfall. They get back around eleven, after seeing more of the sights. I'll get you a schedule of events. We're having a ranch rodeo on Saturday, then cowboy poetry, and a dance. The guests leave on Sunday."

"Sounds like you keep the guests busy."

"That's the goal. We don't want anyone getting bored." Stepping outside, Virgil pointed toward a woman and young boy. "That's Emma and her son, Koa. She works in the kitchen with Nacho. He plans to retire soon. We hope she'll stay on and take over for him. I'll call her over so you can meet her."

Trace turned away, his heart squeezing at the sight of his family. It had been over two years since he'd seen them. He missed them terribly.

"Would you mind if we grabbed a copy of the schedule for me?"

"Sure. You can meet Emma and Koa later. He's nine and a great kid. I would've thought he'd be on the ride this morning. Heckuva rider. Guess his father followed the rodeo, the same as you." Virgil headed toward the main house as he talked, unaware of the affect his words had on Trace.

Keeping his face turned away, he wanted nothing more than to walk straight to Emma, beg her to give him another chance. Taking slow, deep breaths, he shoved the thought from his mind. Sticking to the plan was his path to success with his former wife.

Following Virgil into Wyatt's office, he closed the door. "Here are the schedules for the next month. They're almost identical from week to week. We have to be flexible when weather rolls in. We've done a couple of day programs right here in the main house when storms have come through. Guests don't have to participate. They can stay in their cabins or watch the activities from one of the large, stuffed chairs in the room. Some just sit in front of the fireplace and read or sleep. This is your master key card for the cabins. Don't lose it. They're more complicated to duplicate than individual key cards."

Taking a quick look at it, Trace slid the card into a pocket. "Where do you suggest I start?"

"When the guests return from the morning ride, I'll introduce you. They'll have free time before lunch, which will give you and the other ranch hands time to untack the horses, groom, and feed them. The wagon will also need to be cleaned up."

Trace checked the schedule. "Lunch is at one?"

"Yep. Daisy arrives at three o'clock and teaches a jewelry making class." Virgil mentioned Wyatt's wife who owned a successful artist shop in Brilliance. "It's turned out to be very popular. She also teaches a photography class on Mondays. Men and women like that one."

"What are the kids doing during these classes?"

"My mother, Monica, takes care of their activities. She mixes it up, but usually does a scavenger hunt, a cooking class, which includes Emma, or has one of the ranch hands teach them how to rope a steer. You'll meet her soon."

Trace continued to listen, though the mention of Emma had his mind wandering to the beautiful woman who'd been his wife. Until he messed it up and lost everything important to him.

He had to be careful the next few days. Trace didn't want to reveal himself to Emma or Koa too soon. His son would be glad to see him. Not so much his former wife.

Trace had done some bonehead moves, but not what she'd accused him of. In all their years together, he'd never been unfaithful.

He had been young. Too young to have a kid.

His efforts had been focused on being a rodeo star, with all the benefits which came with it. Trace had always loved the attention, hamming it up for the cameras, having his arm around a pretty one or two. Never had he crossed the line. No matter his protests, Emma hadn't believed him.

After four years of marriage and a young son, she'd left. He didn't blame her. His choices and selfish behavior had pushed her away. By the time he'd realized he was losing his wife, it had been too late.

Five years had passed since the disintegration of their marriage. Close to four since he'd last seen her or Koa.

The accident over a year ago had forced him to make some hard decisions. Changes he should've made years earlier.

Finding her at Whistle Rock Ranch had been a fluke, triggering his application for a job. Regardless of the way it came about, it was his chance, maybe his last, to convince her to give him one more try.

Chapter Two

Emma placed the third load of towels into the dryer, touching the keys to put the level on high. She didn't normally do housework. With the housekeeper home with a cold, Emma had no problem jumping in to help.

She'd been surprised when Koa decided to stay around the house today. He'd looked forward to the ride, spending time with the guests and Wyatt. Then he'd changed his mind. Interesting, as he didn't want to talk about his reasons for staying behind.

Emma didn't have time to dwell on Koa's change of heart. He'd been going nonstop since the first guests arrived a few weeks earlier. Getting up early and going to bed later than normal. Nine-year-olds needed a full night's sleep. She wondered how he'd ever get back on schedule when school started.

"Emma?"

"I'm back here, Nacho. In the laundry room."

"What are you doing, Chica?"

"Eleanor is sick, so I'm helping out. This is the last load, and it's in the dryer. Are you ready for me to start lunch prep?"

He nodded. "We're having those gourmet burgers you suggested. Can you mix up the ground tenderloin and prepare the sauce?"

"I'll get started right away, Nacho. Will you be fixing the guacamole?"

"It's done and in the refrigerator. Lunch is in ninety minutes."

Rushing back to the kitchen, she found Koa standing at the side of a window, peeking out every few seconds.

"What are you looking at?"

Jumping at his mother's question, he clamped his mouth shut.

"Koa?"

"Nothing,"

Brows drawn together, Emma stepped to the window. "It's just the guests returning."

"I know."

She studied him a moment. "All right. If you're not watching something specific, I could use your help in the kitchen."

"But, Mom..."

"It won't take long. Then you can come back and sneak looks at that cute young girl outside."

His mouth twisted in a grimace. "Mom! I'm not watching a girl."

"Maybe not, which means you can help me out. Then you're free to join the others."

"Fine." Head hung low, he trudged toward the big island in the center of the kitchen. "What do you want me to do?"

"Set the tables for lunch. We're using the brightly painted dishware, red handled utensils, and green napkins. Nacho stopped at the new Mexican restaurant in town and bought fresh chips. Set the bags into two large bowls on the buffet table. I'll open them right before lunch. Oh, and get the brioche-style hamburger buns out of the pantry."

"The what?"

"Brioche buns. They're labeled. You can't miss them."

"Right. Is that all?"

"I can come up with more if you want."

"No. Can I start now?"

"Sure. Thanks, Koa."

He looked at his mother as if she were crazy and stomped off to the cupboard holding the dinnerware. It didn't stop him from glancing over his shoulder to look out the window.

Keeping his back to the kitchen, Trace introduced himself to the guests, answering any questions they threw at him. They were a nice group of people from across the United States. One couple had flown in from Sydney, Australia. Everyone seemed to be having a great time, which meant the ranch was exceeding their expectations.

"Lunch will be ready at one o'clock. Daisy Bonner will be here at three for a jewelry making class. She's extremely talented and has a successful shop in town. Ladies, you won't want to miss it. Between now and one, you're free to do whatever you want. Questions?"

When there weren't any, Trace excused himself. Virgil and Wyatt had stood to the side, watching him. As the guests dispersed, Wyatt came up to him.

Wyatt held out his hand. "You did good, Trace."

Clasping it, he acknowledged the praise with a chin lift. "Thanks."

"You'll be joining us inside for lunch. They enjoy eating with the staff."

Controlling a scowl, he nodded.

"Nacho, our longtime cook, and Emma, his assistant, are great."

"I'm sure they are."

"I'll be there, also. Virgil has some other things to take care of and won't be there." Wyatt checked the time. "See you in an hour. It's good to have you here, Trace."

"Thanks. I'm real glad to be working for you." Watching Wyatt walk toward the barn, Trace again made sure his back was to the house.

He didn't know how to get out of lunch, or how he'd avoid Emma. And where would Koa be during lunch? His son spent a lot of time with the guests. Trace had seen several young guests around Koa's age. Would he even remember his father?

Killing the next hour by throwing his meager belongings into the dresser in the bunkhouse and checking on his horse, he considered how to modify what had seemed a solid plan.

It had all seemed so simple. Get a job at the ranch, reconnect with Emma, and over time, get her to trust him again. Rehashing what once sounded logical, now appeared naïve. By the time Trace entered the dining room, he'd revised the original idea.

Joining the guests in the buffet line, he filled a plate while carrying on a conversation with the woman in front of him. About his mother's age, she'd signed up at the encouragement of a girlfriend. They came together and were having a great time. And they'd be attending Daisy's class.

Smiling, he found a seat at a table with two young couples and three middle-aged men. So far, no sign of Emma or Koa. Maybe he'd worried over nothing. He began to relax.

Then she appeared. More beautiful than he remembered. She'd lost weight, and her hair was longer, but it was Emma. A smile graced her features as she set another platter of burgers on the buffet table.

She didn't see him before turning to obtain another platter of food from the kitchen. Setting it beside the burgers, which were already half gone, her gaze scanned the guests. She spent little time on each, passing over Trace without a hint of recognition.

Lowering his head, he didn't see her hesitate before moving back to him. The sharp intake of breath roared through him. Reluctantly, he raised his head to meet the glare of the woman who'd haunted his sleep for years.

Neither spoke, just stared, careful not to draw attention to their personal drama. After a moment, Trace sensed the confusion moving around the table. He couldn't allow it to continue.

"Excellent burgers, ma'am. In fact, it's all wonderful."

He could almost see the wheels spin inside her head. She couldn't leave his comment hanging, not with several guests watching her.

She choked out her response. "Thank you."

Standing, he walked to the buffet table, adding a second burger and another scoop of her incredible macaroni salad to his plate. Careful not to crowd her, he returned to his spot at the table, taking a huge bite of the burger.

He didn't look her way as he listened to the various conversations around him. The shuffling of feet told him Emma had returned to the kitchen. Letting out a shaky breath, he stared at a full plate of food that no longer appealed to him.

"Why does he have to look so good?" Emma mumbled the words as she loaded a tray of homemade desserts.

"Brownies, chocolate chip and oatmeal raisin cookies, lemon squares, and ramekins of chilled flan." She spoke out load, attempting to force thoughts of Trace Griffin from her head.

"Are you all right, Chica?"

Nacho stood at her side, concern etched on his face.

"I'm fine. Just getting the desserts ready."

He eyed the tray. "Uh-huh. Go ahead and take them out."

"Would you mind putting them on the buffet table?"

He studied her a moment. Emma knew Nacho made it a point of not interacting with the guests. He was a cook, not a Chamber of Commerce ambassador.

"You go ahead and take it out. I would need to clean up." Gesturing with his hands, he drew attention to his soiled apron and clothes.

Emma knew he was right. When guests were present, the older man never delivered food to the tables. This had always been her job. Changing the rules now wasn't going to happen.

"All right." Picking up the tray, she thought of Koa and looked around. Where was he? Had he seen Trace? Gripping the tray a little tighter, she delivered it to the dining room, not pausing to glance at the guests.

Except for one, and his seat was empty.

Trace cut a path to a cabin set aside for classes such as Daisy's. A little larger than the others, it was also where the ranch sold products such as t-shirts, hats, jewelry, and framed photography from her art shop.

Entering the cabin, he forced thoughts of Emma and Koa from his mind. What happened next was out of his control. How he responded—that was another matter.

The response occupied his thoughts. He'd made up his mind not to be the one to approach Emma. She'd have to come to him.

Giving her the power to decide if and when they talked was a risk. Like so many times before, she might tuck her feelings inside, hide within herself, refusing to bring up a painful subject.

It had been her usual reaction when they were married. She'd rather pack up and run than be embroiled in conflict. It was why he'd never known the depth of her pain until she'd decided on a divorce.

As he'd been told by several friends, that was his side of the story. He was certain there was another, but Emma never opened up to him. She'd packed her and Koa's belongings, and ran home to her mother.

A mother who disliked cowboys of any kind. Rodeo cowboys in particular. Trace still believed he and Emma may have been able to salvage their marriage if his mother-in-law hadn't encouraged the divorce.

It was this belief which drove him to locate her and try again. Trace knew he may be deceiving himself, but right now, hope was all he had left.

Chapter Three

Koa dashed between the buildings, not wanting his mother or anyone else to know about his father being at the ranch. They couldn't know about the man they'd hired. Koa was certain Wyatt or Virgil would've said something to his mother if they had.

Making his way to the cabin used for classes and selling products, he peaked inside. His father walked around, looking at the t-shirts, hats, blankets, and other items which interested their guests. He looked older than Koa remembered.

But the man was his father. Trace Kekoa Griffin, born of a Hawaiian mother and white father. Koa's grandparents. They lived in Hawaii. Koa thought he remembered them from before his mother decided to move away from his father. He hadn't seen them for a long time.

What Koa did remember was his mother telling him many times about how much he looked like his father. It made him happy to think he did.

Footfalls behind him had Koa rushing to the other side of the cabin. Looking around the corner, he saw Daisy coming toward him carrying two plastic boxes holding supplies for her class. He hoped she hadn't seen him.

"Hello. You must be Trace." Daisy set down her boxes, holding out a hand.

Smiling, he grasped her hand. "And you must be Daisy. It's good to meet you. Can I help you set up?"

"Thanks, but I have a routine. Preparation takes little time. How are you getting along so far?"

"My first day's gone fine. I haven't asked Wyatt and Virgil's opinion, though." He chuckled on the last.

"I'm sure you're doing great." Leaning a hip against a display cabinet, she looked him up and down. "Have we met before?"

"No, ma'am. I would've remembered."

"Sorry. You just look familiar."

"Hello. Hope we aren't too early." The older woman who'd stood in the buffet line with Trace walked in, followed by three other women. "We're all excited about the class today, Daisy." She looked at Trace. "We took her photography class on Monday, and it was fabulous."

"I'm so glad to have you back," Daisy said as she set out more supplies.

More women and a couple men walked in, greeting Daisy before taking seats. She recognized them from Monday's photography class. A good sign.

"I'll leave you to it, Daisy." Trace tipped his hat to the guests.

Looking toward the closest corral, he saw several other guests watch ranch hands rope steers. They weren't on horses. After the demonstration, a few of the guests volunteered to try it. All but one steer was left in the corral.

Three ranch hands kept the animal from running toward the roper while a fourth gave instructions.

Lots of whooping and clapping, along with numerous pictures, accompanied each roper. Trace found himself shouting and laughing with them. Standing on the bottom rail, he rested his arms on the top. He estimated twelve guests stood around the corral, all with broad smiles.

"Were you really a rodeo star?"

Trace looked down at the owner of the small voice. Guessing her to be around ten, he stepped down, then knelt.

"Where did you hear that?"

"My grandpa." She pointed to a man on the other side of the corral. "He said you were the best. He said you were hurt and can't compete anymore. Is that right?"

"I'm afraid so." Trace lowered his voice. "Can I tell you a secret?"

Jaw dropping, she nodded. "Okay."

"I like being here at Whistle Rock Ranch better."

Looking around, the young girl shrugged. "If you say so."

"You're not having a good time?"

"I'm having a great time. It's just...well..." She swiveled the toe of her boot in the dirt. "It can't be the same as being in a rodeo. Right?"

"You're right. The thing is, I rodeoed a long time. My body got tired. Now I'm doing something else I love."

"What's that?"

"Spending time with people like you. People who want to experience ranching."

"Oh." She glanced across the corral. "I better get back to my grandpa."

"What's your name?"

"Alice. But everyone calls me Allie."

Holding out his hand, he gripped her small one. "Nice to meet you, Allie."

She ran off, waving over her shoulder.

Trace watched, chuckling to himself when a second child, a boy, ran toward her. Koa. The chuckle died on his lips as he watched the two children run off to another corral where several horses grazed.

Taking his time, Trace made his way toward them, careful not to show himself to Koa. Leaning against the side of the barn, he crossed his arms and watched.

His son pointed to a small Paint near the center of the pasture. The excitement in his voice carried to where Trace stood.

"That horse is mine." Koa pointed excitedly. "He probably won't grow much more. Virgil trained him for me, so he's real safe to ride. Do you like horses?"

Allie's head bobbed eagerly. "Grandpa said he'll buy me a horse if my parents say it's okay."

"He should buy one of ours because they're the best. Come on." Koa ran off toward the barn, Allie following.

Trace couldn't move for the hurt in his heart. Koa had become his own little man in the last few years, and he'd missed all of it. Blinking back the burning behind his eyes, he swallowed the lump of ice in his throat, making himself a promise.

"I'm not going to miss any more of it."

Emma finished putting away the lunch dishes, her mind divided between dinner prep and the appearance of her ex-husband. The man hadn't changed one bit since she'd last seen him. Just as handsome, and she guessed, as cocky as before.

The anger rose before she could control it. Why was he here? Was he a guest? There'd be no reason for Trace to pay money for a dude ranch experience. Growing up on a big spread, then rodeoing as an amateur and professional, far outweighed what Whistle Rock offered their guests. Which meant?

"No, it couldn't be."

Nacho looked up from where he chopped vegetables for dinner. "Are you talking to me?"

"No. Just wondering about one of the men who came in for lunch. I hadn't noticed him before today."

"I heard Virgil hired someone to ramrod the dude ranch. Some ex-rodeo guy. May have been him."

Her heart sank. "He's going to live and work here?"

Chuckling, Nacho continued his work. "Same as all of us. Eat, sleep, and work here. Why? Does this bother you?"

"It doesn't." But it did bother her. Trace had to know she and Koa were at the ranch when he applied for work.

"The strip steaks are in the refrigerator. Could you please season them for me, and start the carrot soup?" When she didn't respond, Nacho walked toward her. "Emma? Did you hear me?"

A quick shake of her head pulled her away from the dreary thoughts. "I'm sorry. What did you say?"

Repeating his request, she nodded before walking to the large refrigerator. Two large platters of strip steaks were covered with plastic wrap, along with one smaller plate of chicken breasts.

Nacho's recipe was his own, which he'd finally shared with her. Emma had made up a huge batch, good for at least ten meals for dude ranch guests.

Generously sprinkling the steaks and chicken with the mix, she recovered them, slipping the platters back into the refrigerator. Grabbing three bunches of fresh carrots, she sliced off the stems, washing them before loading the food processor.

The soup was another of Nacho's recipes. An old family secret using just enough jalapeños to add some zing. She had to admit it was exceptional.

The back door slammed open, Koa running up to stand beside her.

"Mom! I'm going with Virgil."

"Not until you go back outside and reenter as a gentleman."

"Mooommm, he's getting ready to leave."

"Then you better come back in real quick."

A large groan followed Koa outside. Opening the door, he walked inside, shooting a sly look at Nacho, who winked at him.

"Okay. Now can I go with Virgil?"

"Where to?"

"After strays and fix some fencing."

"You'll stick with Virgil? No riding off by yourself?"

"Yep."

"All right." She bent down to kiss his cheek.

"Mooommm!" But he didn't try wiping the kiss away.

"Be careful, Koa."

"I will." Waving, he dashed outside, allowing the door to slam behind him.

She watched him race toward the barn, her mouth agape.

"He's a good boy, Emma."

"I know, Nacho." Tucking hair behind her ear, she let out a sigh. "There is so much more to think about as they get older. I don't want to make a mistake."

Turning to face her, he waved the knife in the air. "You love and worry about him. Nothing wrong with that. The boy's got a bunch of 'uncles' on the ranch. No one's going to let anything happen to him."

"They're working. They can't watch Koa all the time."

"A boy needs space. Especially a kid like Koa. He has a lot of energy. It's good he loves the outdoors." Turning back to the bowls of vegetables, he began humming, ending their conversation.

Emma tried to concentrate on the carrot soup they'd be serving for dinner. She felt unsettled, unable to keep her mind on what needed to get done. Blaming Koa would be easy but incorrect. What weighed on her couldn't be blamed on a nine-year-old boy.

The cause of her unease stood over six feet, with sculpted muscles from years working with horses and competing in rodeos. A man she'd loved with her entire being. Still loved him. Had never found a way to stop.

Now he was here, on the ranch, where she'd see him every day. Koa hadn't said anything, yet it wouldn't be long before he recognized Trace as his father.

Then what would she do?

Chapter Four

"Jasper!" Virgil's father shifted in his saddle, watching the most beautiful woman in the world run up to him. She held something in her hand.

"You forgot your inhaler." Grabbing his hand, she slipped the device into his palm. "Don't lose it." A broad smile came with the warning.

"Thank you." Slipping it into a pocket, he leaned down for a kiss. "We shouldn't be gone long."

Virgil watched the exchange between his parents, as did Barrel, Koa, and three other ranch hands. They'd reunited after many years apart, yet their status was still a mystery to most, including their son.

Virgil had married the love of his life, Lily, a few weeks earlier. They'd had their troubles, too, and he still couldn't quite believe they'd been able to forge a future together.

"Pop, you ride up front with Barrel. And don't be stubborn. Use the inhaler if you need to." Jasper had been diagnosed with late onset adult asthma a few months earlier.

Now regulated with medications and a few changes in his routine, the asthma seemed under control. Or would be if Jasper remembered to keep his inhaler with him.

"Koa, you stay with me. Get no more than a dozen feet away."

"Okay, Virgil." Shifting in the saddle, Koa looked for his female golden lab. "Trooper!" Seconds later, the dog came storming around the barn, running in circles around Koa and his horse.

The foreman glanced around the small group. "All right. Let's get this done."

Jeramy Barrel headed west, then north, leading them in the direction of the broken fence. He'd spotted the opening the evening before while looking for stray cattle. Too big a job to complete before dark, he'd decided to return today with more men. They'd repair the breaks and search for any missing steers.

"You got Emma's permission to ride along, right, Koa?"

Riding not more than three feet away from Virgil, he nodded. "Yes. She said I had to stay near you."

"Then we've both told you the same thing. I'll be busy, so it'll be up to you not to wander away."

"All right." Koa laughed as Trooper started her usual antics of running in small circles, as if encouraging the riders to speed up.

Virgil cast a sideways look at the boy. He saw a lot of himself and Wyatt in the adventurous lad. Always on the go, ready for anything, everyone enjoyed watching Koa.

They rode for almost an hour before Barrel raised a hand to show the break in the fence. Dismounting, they removed tools and lengths of wire from custom designed saddlebags. They'd return on four wheelers Sunday, during the turnover in guests, to make permanent fixes.

While Barrel and the ranch hands completed the temporary repairs, Virgil, Koa, and Jasper looked for strays or anything suspicious. They weren't at the westernmost boundary of the ranch, but it was as far as Koa had ever ridden.

Sitting in the saddle, the young boy stared at the majestic Tetons. "They're so big."

"They are," Virgil responded. "When the dude ranch season is over, maybe we can talk Wyatt into a short camping trip."

Koa's face brightened. "Really? That would be awesome!" Looking down at his hands wrapped around the saddlehorn, he shot a sheepish look at Virgil. "Maybe we can invite the new ranch hand."

"The new hand? Did you meet him?"

"No. I saw him walking around today."

Virgil stretched his legs so he stood in the stirrups. Scanning the area, he sat down. "We'll see. I won't make any promises." He glanced at his father, who'd positioned himself on the other side of Koa. "Let's ride a little farther north before returning to the fence."

The trail didn't change much from where they'd started. Flat, winding, and narrow. Virgil opened a gate, which led them into another pasture. Considerably larger than the previous one, there were no cattle grazing.

When Trooper ran ahead, barking, something caught Virgil's attention.

"Pop. Over there." He pointed to Trooper and a lump on the ground a few feet away from the lab.

Jasper rode toward the odd-shaped mound, reining up when several feet away. Without dismounting, he rode around what he believed to be a dead calf. At the sound of horses behind him, Jasper glanced over his shoulder, raising a hand to keep them from getting too close.

"Wait here, Koa." Virgil moved toward the object, stopping next to his father. "A calf?"

"Believe so."

"Looks mutilated." Virgil rode a little closer. "There appears to be a Whistle Rock brand, but I can't be sure. What would do something like this?"

Jasper shook his head, both men unaware Koa had ridden forward.

"Ew. What is it?"

Virgil held up his hand. "Don't get too close and stay on your horse. Trooper, you go with Koa." The lab did as ordered.

His features scrunched up, mouth twisting in disgust. "But what is it?"

"We aren't sure," Jasper answered. "Maybe a calf."

Face turning a greenish shade, Koa reined around, moving several feet away. He whistled for Trooper to stay close.

Sliding his phone from a pocket, Virgil took several pictures from different angles. "I want Wyatt to see these."

"A rabid animal?"

"I don't know, Pop. Could be anything. Maybe the calf died of disease, then was attacked by bugs or other animals. I'll have Barrel come out tomorrow and pick up the carcass. We'll need the vet to determine what happened."

Jasper continued to stare at the inert animal. "It's been here for a while. The smell isn't as bad as a new kill."

"Can we go now, Virgil?" Koa looked better than a few minutes earlier. His face not so green, his breathing more steady.

"Yes, we can. Stay near me or Jasper. Right?"

"I will." Koa's voice had lost most of the excitement.

"It's another lesson, son," Jasper said. "Being a rancher means facing the death of animals more often than we'd like."

Koa didn't respond. Instead, he slotted his horse between Virgil and Jasper, saying little on the ride home.

Monica unwrapped pieces of jewelry Daisy dropped off for the dude ranch, placing each in one of the display cases. Each one a custom piece. All beautiful.

Sales in the gift shop had far exceeded anyone's expectations, necessitating the order of additional products. Hats and jewelry were the biggest sellers, with t-shirts coming in third. All clothing included the custom designed ranch logo.

Next year, Monica would add a cookbook of Nacho's recipes, aprons fitting anyone, and tote bags to the merchandise. All three had been mentioned numerous times on guest surveys.

Attaching the sales price to the last piece of jewelry, her ears picked up the sound of riders. Locking the case, Monica moved to the open doorway, a soft grin lifting the corners of her face. There were days she still couldn't quite believe she lived on the ranch with Jasper and Virgil. Until recently, she'd been banned from visiting her son. There were still unresolved issues, but her life now was vastly different from a year earlier.

Closing and locking the door, she walked out to meet the riders, noting the serious expressions on each face. Virgil slid to the ground, nodding at his mother before striding to meet Wyatt, who approached from the closest corral. After a brief discussion, he walked with Jasper toward his mother.

Monica clasped her hands together, waiting for them. "What happened?"

Jasper reached out, pulling her hands apart and threading his fingers through one of hers. "We found a dead calf. What was left, well...it's not in good shape. Barrel will be bringing it back here tomorrow before delivering it to Dr. Worrel."

"Why not the game and fish warden?"

"We need to know if the calf died from disease." Jasper squeezed his wife's hand.

"I need to find the new man." Virgil scanned the area. "I'm going to send him out with Barrel tomorrow. He might pick up on something we missed. I'll see you two later."

Monica waited until her son was out of hearing distance. "What do you know about the new man?"

"Me? Nothing. Wyatt and Virgil brought him in to ramrod the dude ranch. Have you had a run-in with him?"

"Not at all. Do not think I'm paranoid, but have you noticed the resemblance between Trace and Koa?"

Jasper rubbed his stubbled jaw, mouth twisting as he considered her question. "I suppose there are some similarities."

"From what I understand, Trace was a rodeo star. So was Koa's father. Do you know his last name?"

"Not a clue. I also don't know Emma's. Everyone goes by their first name." Jasper glanced toward the kitchen's back door. "Has she said anything to you?"

"No, and I'm not going to ask her. I'm curious is all."

Jasper thought about the quiet cook. She did her work without complaint, was pleasant to everyone, and worked well with Nacho. Not an easy task. The crusty, longtime cook had caused more than one assistant to run off in frustration. Not Emma. Her calm, competent manner worked well with Nacho's brusque exterior.

Massaging the back of his neck, Jasper continued to think about the possibility Emma's ex-husband had been hired to work at the ranch. They couldn't afford to lose her, and from what Virgil had shared, he and Wyatt were happy with the new man.

Placing an arm around Monica's shoulders, he hugged her to him. "Maybe you should talk to Emma."

"And say what? Hey, your son looks a lot like the new hire?"

"Why not? Don't women talk to each other about this sort of stuff?"

"Jasper, there are times when you can be so dense." Blowing out a breath, she considered his suggestion. "I'm probably making an issue out of nothing. Let's forget I said anything."

"If you're sure?"

"I am. From the little I know about her marriage, it wasn't real amicable. If that is Koa's father, Emma will say something to Wyatt or Virgil, or maybe Daisy. She won't be able to ignore his presence. Especially not when Koa realizes who the man is."

Jasper remembered what he'd heard from the boy about inviting Trace to go along on a camping trip. Koa was a bright boy. It wouldn't be a stretch to discover he'd already figured out the new man was his father.

Chapter Five

Trace finished dinner with the guests, leaving before dessert to help prepare for the evening campfire program. Barrel and another ranch hand would be reading cowboy poetry. Then they'd join three others to lead group sing-a-longs while roasting s'mores, making it an early night.

Tomorrow, Wyatt's youngest brother, Gage, would be taking most of the guests hiking. Along the way, they'd gather wild berries. Nacho would use them to make pies for dinner on the last night.

Voices surged from the open doors of the main ranch house, the guests streaming toward the already blazing fire. Among them, two small figures ran toward Trace.

Koa, holding something in his hand, and Allie laughed as Trooper raced around them. Stopping in front of Trace, Koa held out something inside a napkin.

"This is for you."

The lump in Trace's throat swelled. This was the first time Koa had spoken to him in over three years. Taking it from his son's hand, he peeled back the covering to see a chocolate chip cookie.

"You didn't get dessert before you left," Koa explained while digging the toe of his boot into the dirt. Beside him, Allie petted Trooper, her gaze on the flickering flames.

"This is great." Taking a bite, Trace gave a moan of satisfaction. "Thank you. Did your mother make this?"

"She bakes all the cookies and brownies. Sometimes, she also makes the pies. Do you want another one?"

"This one is fine. Maybe later I'll go search for another." Throat dry, Trace found it hard to swallow from the emotion raging inside him.

"Come on, Koa. Let's go find seats." Allie's impatience didn't move Koa.

"Go ahead. I'll be there in a minute."

"Okay." Running off, she glanced over her shoulder before slowing near the campfire.

Staring up at Trace, Koa's features took on a determined look. "You're my dad."

Stilling with the cookie partway to his mouth, Trace gave an almost imperceptible nod. "Yes, I am."

"I thought so." Switching his attention to the ground, Koa grew quiet.

Kneeling, Trace used a finger under Koa's chin to get his son's attention. "I came here to see you."

A smile broke across his face. "You did?"

"I did."

Unable to hold back any longer, Koa launched himself into Trace's arms. "I knew it."

Holding on tight, he rubbed his son's back. "I missed you."

"Me too." Slipping out of his father's arms, he took a small step backward. "Mom is going to be mad."

"About what?"

"You being here."

"I see." Trace felt regret swamping him. He'd handled the separation and divorce wrong, giving up his parental rights and agreeing to stay away from Koa. But he wasn't the same man now. "Maybe your mom and I should talk."

Pursing his lips, Koa cast a look toward the house. "That might be good."

"Hey, Trace!"

Both he and Koa looked in the direction of the voice to see Virgil waving at him.

"We could use your help."

"Be right there." Standing, he set a hand on his son's shoulder and squeezed. "I don't want you to worry. I'll find a way to make this work. Okay?"

The hopeful smile almost broke Trace's heart. "Okay, Dad."

Jaw clenched, arms crossed over her chest, Emma stood at the window, watching Koa and Trace. Her son and her former husband. The man who didn't fight for his family, who wasn't ready for children, who gave up his rights as a father.

To be fair, also a man who sent money every month, even though she never asked for it and the court didn't require it. Watching the two, the pain in her chest intensified.

"Are you all right, Emma?" Monica joined her at the window, following the direction of her gaze. "Virgil and Wyatt are quite happy with the new man. Looks like Koa might feel the same."

A sob burst from Emma's throat. Covering her face, she started to turn away, stilling when Monica gripped her shoulders, drawing her into a hug. She said nothing, letting Emma cry out whatever plagued her. Monica had a good idea, deciding to keep it to herself.

Sniffling, Emma stepped away. "I'm sorry."

"Why? We all need a good cry once in a while."

"I suppose so. It's just, well...I never cry." Swiping at her damp face, she grabbed a tissue from a nearby table. "This is a little embarrassing."

"No reason for you to be embarrassed, Emma. Seeing your son and former husband together has to be an adjustment."

Emma whipped toward Monica. "What?"

"Anyone with two good eyes can see Koa is a miniature of Trace."

"I didn't realize how much until tonight. Seeing them together, the happiness on both their faces..." Emma gave a slow shake of her head. "Doesn't matter. None of us can go back and change what happened."

"Are you sure? Seems to me you and Trace can control your future."

"You don't understand. I don't want to go back to the way it was, and trusting him again isn't an option."

Monica turned to look out the window. "He cheated on you?"

"He always denied it, but a friend told me she saw him with someone." Covering her face with both hands, Emma groaned. "My mother believed he cheated."

"What did you believe?"

Face twisting into a grim expression, Emma crossed her arms around her waist in a protective stance. "Mom said I'd be stupid to believe he didn't cheat."

"I see."

"She's done so much for me and Koa, I felt she deserved my loyalty." Licking her lips, Emma looked more miserable than thankful.

"Well, there's nothing you can do about the past. As for the present, you'll have to make a decision how much you'll allow Trace into your life, and Koa's."

"Oh, I have no intention of allowing him back into my life." Sighing, she looked out the window. "Koa is at an age where he needs his father."

"Is there a reason he can't spend time with Trace without you having to interact with your husband much?"

"Ex-husband," Emma corrected.

"Right. If you need a go-between, I'd be happy to help you."

"You do so much for everyone already, Monica. I couldn't ask you to get between Trace and me."

"That's not how I see it. I wouldn't be getting between anyone. However, I do believe the best way to handle this is for the two of you to find a way to talk without digging up the past."

"You're right, it's just..." A wistful expression appeared before Emma turned back to the window.

"What you're facing isn't easy. He's been out of your lives for years, then shows up at the ranch. If it's too much, I could talk to Virgil or Wyatt about firing him."

"No! I mean, he probably needs the work. And I truly do want Trace and Koa to get to know each other."

A compassionate smile grew on Monica's face. "You don't have to decide anything tonight. Take time to think about what you want to do. Trace isn't going anywhere, and neither are you."

It was good advice. "All right. There's no reason to make a quick decision."

"I'll leave you alone. There's much you have to consider." Placing a hand on Emma's shoulder, Monica squeezed lightly. "I'm always here if you want to talk."

Nodding, her mouth drew into a thin line as she continued watching her son and his father. So much about them was similar. Their laugh, smile, gestures. The color of their hair and eyes. Both were expressive, using their hands when talking.

Tears burned at the back of her eyes. She wanted to feel happy they'd reconnected. The excitement on Koa's face told the entire story. He wanted Trace in his life. How could she come between them?

Unable to watch any longer, she headed to the kitchen. Nacho had already retreated to his room. Emma often took this time to do prep for breakfast. She didn't have the energy for much of anything tonight.

Leaving on the light over the prep counter, she headed to her living quarters at the back of the house. The Bonners provided two bedrooms with an adjoining bath for her and Koa. She had full use of the kitchen on her days off and after work hours.

Looking around the rooms which had become her refuge, a safe place for her and Koa, she sat down on an overstuffed chair. It and another one faced a wall mounted screen. Her life shifted between these living quarters and the kitchen.

Emma couldn't recall the last time she'd been off the ranch. She and Nacho wrote out what they needed, and gave the list to Jasper, who made sure the supplies were delivered. Her days off were filled with laundry, cleaning their rooms, and spending time with Koa.

When was the last time she did anything for herself? She couldn't come up with anything.

Trace sat next to his son, watching the ranch hands entertain the guests. He wouldn't have guessed there'd be so much talent in the circle of men across the campfire.

Every few minutes, he'd cast a look toward the house, wondering if Emma might be watching them. When their eyes had locked at lunch, Trace was certain she'd hunt him down, demand he leave the ranch. The fact she hadn't puzzled him.

"Does your mother ever sit around the campfire with everyone else?"

Koa shook his head. "Nah. She works all the time."

"Does she ever get off the ranch?"

"Nope. Well, maybe sometimes. We go to church sometimes, but it has been a while." Koa didn't move his attention from the performers. "You could take her somewhere."

"I doubt she'll let me get close enough to ask. Does she ever talk about me?"

"No."

The answer didn't surprise him. What would she tell Koa? Whatever Emma said wouldn't be good, even if it was the truth.

Deciding nothing could be decided tonight, Trace watched the cowboys finish their routine. Emma wasn't going anywhere, and neither was he. There was time. Lots and lots of time.

Chapter Six

"Thanks for coming into town for this." Doctor Dorie Worrel led Virgil and Wyatt to the back room where she performed animal forensics. Turning down a hallway, they entered her office. "Sit down, guys." Picking up a folder, she opened it, turning it to face them. "This one was a little more complicated due to the condition of the carcass."

Wyatt and Virgil exchanged looks as they studied the forensic images. The label of each identified the animal as a calf.

"I'm estimating the age to be between forty-five and sixty days old."

"Weaned?" Wyatt asked.

"That's my assumption. I believe the calf contracted bovine respiratory disease. The causal agents are multiple, such as bacteria, virus, and fungus. This poor thing didn't have a chance. Deterioration was quick. Animals got to him, doing the rest of the damage."

Wyatt pushed the file back to her. "I've got men looking for other infected calves."

Setting the file aside, she clasped her hands together on the top of her desk. "I'd like to come out and inspect the herd."

"Whenever it's convenient for you," Wyatt said. "One of us will go with you."

Dorie checked her computer screen. "I can come by this afternoon. Sometime around two, if that works for you."

"It works. Will checking the closest herd be all right? Checking all the cattle will take more than one visit."

"No worries, Wyatt. I'll start with the herd closest to the house. If I find anything, I'll need to check the entire herd." Shoving her chair back, she stood. "Unless you have any concerns about the autopsy, I'll dispose of the carcass."

Wyatt rose. "No concerns, doc. Thanks for getting to this so quickly."

"The dead calf was a priority. I'll see you guys this afternoon."

Trace didn't know how he'd gotten roped into participating in Gage's hiking trip. He'd been reading off the events of the day to a group of guests, when a few of them asked him to come along. Trying to get out of it didn't work, as there were plenty of employees to help with activities for those choosing not to join the hikers.

Years had passed since he'd hiked anything steeper than his trailer's ramp. He was a man who stayed in shape for riding broncs, both bareback and saddle. It didn't take long for him to realize the muscles used in the rodeo didn't translate to mountain trails.

When his calves began to tighten at the same time his knees felt as if they'd blow out, Trace knew he was in trouble. He should've known his knees would betray him.

The injury during his last ride included blowing out both knees. They were the prime reason he'd never compete again. Sustaining more damage to his already ravaged knees ran the risk of him never walking again. There'd really been no choice at all.

Gage's voice wafted over the line of hikers until reaching Trace. "All right, everyone. We have one last fifty yard trail and we'll be at the summit. Anyone want to rest?"

Thankfully, Trace didn't have to raise his hand. Three other hikers beat him to it. Finding a spot to rest just off the trail and away from the others, he pulled a bag of ice from his backpack. Holding it to one knee, then the other, he knew he'd failed Gage. The youngest Bonner walked among the hikers, handing out energy bars and offering bottles of water.

"Do you need some aspirin?"

Trace looked into the eyes of an older man at least twenty years older than him. When he opened his mouth to decline, the man held out two tablets.

"I know about your injury during a rodeo a while back. This hike can't be doing those knees any good."

Feeling heat climb up his face, Trace held out his hand. "Thanks, sir." Popping them into his mouth, he swallowed several gulps of water.

Lowering himself next to Trace, the man looked over the group. "Most of these people hike often. You can tell by their clothes and shoes. When was the last time you climbed a mountain?"

Choking out a laugh, Trace shook his head. "High school. Maybe before then. Most of my free time was spent working my parents' ranch and practicing for rodeo events. You follow rodeo?"

"Sure do. I grew up north of Yellowstone in Montana. Never competed myself, but loved watching. Followed you from the time you started until that last ride."

Trace had spoken with few fans who actually watched the events. Most often, it would be buckle bunnies who followed the cowboys from one rodeo to the next, and they weren't interested in how the cowboys did in the arena.

"That last ride still plays in my dreams. It's for the best, though."

Brows drawing together, the man cocked his head. "How so?"

"It was time. There were things I needed to fix."

"That's what you've been doing?"

"I'm getting there."

Clasping Trace on the shoulder, he stood, taking a card from his pocket. "I'm an orthopedic surgeon in Jackson. You make an appointment and come see me. No cost for the exam and consultation. I may be able to help you out."

Before Trace could respond, the man jogged to the front of the line. Standing, he glanced at the card before tucking it into a pocket. Maybe he would call.

The insurance he had during his run in the circuit was good, and he'd had adequate care after his injury.

Adequate. That was the word his mother used to describe the doctor. She'd never come right out and said she thought Trace could do better. Still, the vibe was there. Maybe he would make a trip to Jackson to see what the man could do.

The aspirin worked some, but by the time the group returned, both knees were swollen to the size of grapefruits. At least his jeans hid them from the hikers. Only the doctor had commented.

"Dad!" Koa's excited voice hit him square in the gut. *Dad.* It had been way too long since he'd heard the word. "Where'd you go?"

"I helped Gage with the hikers. What did you do today?"

"Me and Allie roped steers. Real ones."

"That's great."

"Yeah. Her grandpa did real good. He said we'd be welcome at their ranch anytime. I, uh…told him you were my dad. Was that all right?"

Trace didn't know what Emma would say about it, but he was fine with it. "Sure. I need to sit down for a bit. Do you want to come with me to the bunkhouse?"

Jumping up and down, Koa grinned. Trace took it as a yes.

The bunkhouse was almost empty when they arrived. Lowering himself onto his bed, he stretched out his legs on a deep moan. Koa sat down on a trunk, facing his father.

"When are you going to tell Mom who you are?"

And there it was. The question had hung between them for a couple days, neither mentioning it until now. "I don't know. Soon."

"Maybe she already knows." Koa rocked back and forth, watching his father.

"Why do you say that?"

"I see her watching us from the kitchen window. She knows, Dad."

Koa was a very sharp kid. Trace had hoped Emma would come to him, make the first move. How long should he wait before approaching her?

"You need to talk to her so I can stay with you."

Trace's chest squeezed. So this was about a son wanting to openly spend time with his father. Maybe staying in the bunkhouse, going camping together, and on long trail rides. Just the two of them, with no other ranch hands around. He wondered what the chances were that Emma would allow them to do this?

What if he approached her with that one request and nothing more? Asked her permission for Koa to spend the night in the bunkhouse. Little steps, as his mother would say.

He could speak with her after dinner, waiting until all the guests had gone outside. Assuming he could get her to talk. There was a good chance Emma would ignore him, pretend he didn't exist, as she'd done the last few years.

Trace still had half a dozen letters she'd returned. He'd always assumed Emma had sent them back. The more he thought about it, and knowing she'd been at Whistle Rock for a couple years, he wondered if her mother had sent them back. Could be Emma never knew he sent them.

"I'll give it a try." First, he'd have to say something to Virgil.

"You should've told me during the interview." Virgil's features had hardened at the news of Trace's relationship with Emma and Koa. "Did you know they were here when you applied?'

"Yes, sir. I'd heard from a friend of mine who knows one of your ranch hands."

Standing, Virgil paced to the window of Wyatt's office before whipping around to glare at Trace. "I should fire you right off."

"Yes, sir."

"Is that what you want?"

"Not at all. The work is great, and so are the people."

Shaking his head in frustration, Virgil sat back down, resting his arms on Wyatt's desk. "Tell me your story. From the start. Don't leave anything out."

"It's your basic failed marriage story. We married young. The rodeo circuit puts a huge strain on marriages. I worked hard. Real hard, practicing early and staying late. That's the reason I rose to the top so quickly. Why I stayed there." Scrubbing both hands over his face, he looked past Virgil to an oil painting of the Tetons.

"Emma could never understand it. Then she got pregnant with Koa. Neither of us were ready, but you do your best. At least I thought that's what I was doing. Turns out she'd been told I was fooling around with the buckle bunnies. A *friend* of hers told Emma she'd seen me with someone. It was a lie. Never, not once, in our years together, did I cheat on her. I may not have been the best husband, but I was never with another woman. She wouldn't listen to me. I came home early one evening, hoping to get her to see my side, but she and Koa were gone."

"Where'd they go?"

"To her mother's place. The woman never liked me. She tried to get Emma to leave me several times while we were married. I should've seen it coming."

"Did you go after her?"

"I did. Pauline, that's Emma's mother, refused to let me in the house. Wouldn't tell Emma I was there. A few weeks passed before divorce papers arrived." He could feel his face heat, felt hot tears at the back of his eyes.

"So you came here to?"

"Try to get Emma to talk to me. At least get her to approve me visiting with my son. That's why I'm telling you. I want to talk to Emma tonight after dinner."

"You say she knows you're here?"

"Yes, she knows."

"I don't want to lose Emma. Nor do I want to lose you. But if she comes to me and insists I let you go, I will. Do you understand this?"

"I understand, Virgil. This job is important to me, but Emma would be real hard to replace."

Slapping a hand on the desk, Virgil's jaw tightened. "Wyatt may decide to let you go, anyway. Nothing I can do about that. It will all come down to what Emma wants."

Tapping down the fear building in his gut, Trace nodded.

"All right. Get out of here and let me go talk to Wyatt. If he disagrees with what I've said, I'll let you know during dinner. Fair enough?"

"More than fair."

Standing, Virgil stalked to the office door and drew it open. "Nothing's ever easy, is it, Trace?"

"No, sir. Nothing in my life anyway."

Chapter Seven

"This isn't what I expected, Virgil. Trace is doing well and the guests love him. Now this." Wyatt finished untacking his horse, setting the saddle on a nearby stand. "Letting him go will be problematic, but upsetting Emma would be worse. What do you suggest?"

"Trace says she's aware of him working here. She hasn't confronted him or kept Koa away from him, which is interesting. I got the impression their divorce was pushed along by Emma's mother."

"You're saying she let herself be led into ending the marriage?"

"I don't have an answer for you, Wyatt. We should talk to her."

"What if we do nothing? Why can't we let them work it out between them? It's not our job to get involved in personal issues."

Stalking a few feet away, Virgil rested fisted hands on his hips before turning back to face Wyatt. "You're right. What if I tell Trace we'll be stepping back to let him and Emma work things out?"

"I have no problem with him telling Emma we know about their past."

Virgil offered a slow nod. "Right. Do you think the men will be all right with him once they learn of the divorce?"

Wyatt waved off his concern. "Our men will be fine. If Trace and Emma don't make a big deal of their past, neither will anyone else." Checking the time, he blew out a tired breath. "Doc Worrel will be here in a few hours."

"Two o'clock. The guests will be into whatever afternoon activity they selected. I'll talk to Trace, then grab one of the ranch hands so we're ready to go when Dorie gets here. It shouldn't take more than an hour for her to check the cattle. Trace will go about his business with the guests. It'll be up to him to decide when to speak with Emma."

"I should probably go with you."

"You have other matters to tackle. Such as your parents returning from their trip later this afternoon."

Slapping a hand against his forehead, Wyatt chuckled. "I forgot they were flying back in today."

"You could send a ranch hand to pick them up. They're flying into Jackson Hole, aren't they?"

"Yeah, but I need to be there for them. After weeks away, Pop is going to want an update from me. I'd rather do it on the drive, than have to meet while our guests are here. I'll need to leave about the time Dorie is supposed to arrive at the ranch."

"Don't worry about it. Between me, Barrel, Jasper, and Trace, we've got everything covered. I'd better get going. I want to speak with Trace before lunch."

Wyatt walked with Virgil out the large barn doors. "Let me know how he responds."

Trace worked alongside Barrel and several other men to prepare for the night's entertainment. The ranch hands would be presenting their own rodeo in the largest corral for the final evening.

Employees would compete in steer wrestling, team roping, bareback riding, and saddle bronc riding. Guests had the opportunity to sign up for steer roping, and children could take part in the mutton bustin' event. The rodeo had been a hit since first introduced during the dude ranch's opening.

"Dad! Where do you want these?" Koa stood a few feet away with a closed box. Inside were numbers the competitors used during professional rodeos. Until now, the men hadn't worn them. Trace had talked a longtime colleague into rounding up older numbers and sending them FedEx to the ranch.

Jogging over, he took the box from Koa's outstretched hands. "Thanks."

"What is it?"

"A surprise for the rodeo competitors."

Koa's eyes lit up. "Including me?"

"Are you competing?"

"I'm doing the mutton bustin'."

Trace chuckled at his son's excitement. "Then you'll get one."

"Are you going to compete?"

"Maybe another time." But Trace doubted it. He'd participated in his fair share of rodeos. They were now out of his reach. "I believe we're about done here. If I remember right, your mother sets out cookies right about now. Race you to the house to get one." He took off without waiting for Koa.

"Hey!" Short legs pumping, he caught up to Trace, passing him as they neared the big house. Touching the back door, he jumped up and down, arms in the air. "I won!"

"You sure did." Opening the door, Trace relaxed at seeing at least a dozen guests already inside. Drinking coffee, tea, or the wine offered every afternoon, they stood in small groups nibbling on cookies, banana or zucchini bread. The room buzzed with energy.

"Oh, good. We hoped you'd show up, Trace." The older woman who always seemed to show up at meals, hustled up beside him. "We're having a discussion on who's competing in the rodeo. I assured them you'd participate. Was I right?"

"Afraid not, ma'am."

"Well, why not?"

"They've got me organizing and supervising the events. Besides, these old bones have been beaten up pretty good over the years."

"Oh? Were you injured?" The concern in her voice touched him.

"I've broken about every bone there is, ma'am. The doctor finally told me I might be crippled for life if I continued."

"Well, then, you shouldn't even consider competing any longer. Your brain is more valuable than your bones." The serious expression had him chuckling.

"I made the same decision."

Patting his arm, she turned toward her group of friends. "I'm sure we'll talk again before I leave tomorrow."

He touched the brim of his hat. "I'll look forward to it, ma'am."

"Here, Dad." Koa held out a napkin with a chocolate chip cookie and brownie. "These are yours."

"Thanks, son."

"Want me to get you coffee?"

"This is fine. What do you have there?" He looked at the huge cookie on Koa's napkin.

"It's a cowboy cookie with candies in the dough. Mom always makes them on the last night. Want a bite?"

"Sure." Bending down, he took a small bite and chewed. "Wow. That's great." Rising, he stilled when his gaze landed on Emma.

Straightening, neither looked away. Taking a few tentative steps, he moved toward her, cookie and brownie still in his hand. He saw the instant Emma saw the napkin, her mouth curving upward ever so slightly.

Stopping several feet away, he cleared his throat. "Hello, Emma."

Lips curling inward, she gave the barest of nods. "Trace."

Holding up his hand, he showed her the half-eaten cookie. "These are excellent."

"Thank you."

"I gave him a bite of the cowboy cookie, Mom. He liked it too."

Smiling at Koa, she returned her attention to Trace. "I understand you're working here."

"Yes. I'd like to stay, assuming you're comfortable with me being here."

She didn't answer. "I have work to do for dinner. Koa, do you want to help or stay with your father?"

Looking between his parents, he appeared conflicted until Trace offered the solution.

"You've spent most of the day with me. Why don't you give your mother some time?"

Relief washed over Koa. "Okay. See you at dinner."

Trace's heart pounded, watching Koa and his mother return to the kitchen. He wanted to go with them, but that day could be a long way off. For now, he'd be content with Emma not being hostile to his presence.

Moving toward the small groups of people, he spoke to several of the guests, asking questions about their stay at the ranch. All were pleased with the experience, and most hoped to return. The differences showed when they talked of what they enjoyed the most.

Some preferred the trail rides. Others enjoyed the hiking and river rafting, both run by Gage. Daisy's classes were very popular, as were the nightly campfires and entertainment. After tonight, he suspected the ranch rodeo would make its way onto the list of favorites.

Checking the time, he moved so everyone could hear him. "Time to finish up and get ready for the final activities before dinner. For those going on the trail ride, meet me at the large stable in fifteen minutes."

As the guests filtered outside, Trace cast a brief look toward the kitchen. The first encounter with Emma went well. Better than he'd hoped. She was more tolerant than friendly. This may have been due to Koa or the guests not more than fifteen feet away. Whatever the reason, it gave Trace reason to believe they may be able to talk, work out some issues without the anger of the past.

Forcing himself to concentrate on the present, he headed outside, walking to the barn stabling the guest horses. There were eighteen guests signed up for the last ride of their dude ranch experience.

Barrel, Jimmy French, and Owen Baker, a married ranch hand with two children, already had most of the horses tacked up and ready for their riders. Trace joined them as they finished, whipping around at the shouted voice of his son.

"Dad! I want to go with you." Breathing hard, he stared up at his father. "Mom said I could."

Stifling a chuckle, Trace pointed to Koa's horse at the far end of the stable. "You'd better get him ready. We leave in fifteen minutes."

"I'll be ready."

Saddling his own horse, Trace brought it around to where the guests waited. "Barrel, Jimmy, and Owen will show you to your horse. Once mounted, come out here with me. This will continue until everyone going on the ride has a horse. I'll take the lead, Barrel will be at the back. Jimmy and Owen will rotate among you. Let them know if there's anything you need. We will be gone a little more than an hour. You'll be back in plenty of time for dinner and tonight's rodeo. Are there questions?"

When none came, he counted the guests. Eighteen. As he finished, Koa rode up beside him.

"Looks like we're all here. Let's ride!"

Chapter Eight

Emma watched out the kitchen window as Trace, with Koa beside him, led the group on their final ride. The last night often elicited strong emotions from their guests. Lots of hugs, thanks, and promises to return. It was always the same, and Emma enjoyed every minute.

Resuming dinner preparations, she turned the marinating steaks, sausages, and chicken, moving on to the potatoes and vegetable skewers. Nacho put the final touches on the appetizers and checked the desserts. If it were up to Emma, she'd eat appetizers and desserts, going to bed a happy woman.

She smiled at the idea of an evening alone, sipping hot chocolate while eating whatever she craved. How long had it been since she had such an evening? Checking the potatoes, she thought of Mack.

It had been a week since she'd spoken to the neighboring rancher. Tall and muscular, with black hair turning to premature silver, the man wore his age well. Nacho had told her Mack was in his forties with two grown sons. His wife had passed five years earlier, and according to town gossip, he'd decided to open his heart a second time. For now, he'd turned his interest on Emma.

"Emma. I meant to tell you Mack stopped by earlier to speak with Anson. Told me he'd be calling you soon."

Her heart didn't skip at the news, yet she felt an undercurrent of anticipation. "Thanks, Nacho."

Mack had taken her to dinner twice over the last couple months. She had a wonderful time, finding him to be excellent company. Perhaps, over time, their feelings would deepen. For now, both seemed content being in each other's company.

Complicating her life was Trace's return. He'd been the love of her life, until his behavior caused suspicion in her mind. When a friend informed Emma of his cheating, she'd jumped on it as a reason to leave. His denying the accusations hadn't impacted her decision, not with her mother pushing her to get a divorce. Years later, looking at their past from a more mature perspective, Emma wondered if she'd made a huge mistake.

"How's the meat?"

Shaking off thoughts of Trace, Emma checked the large glass baking pans. "They're ready, as are the potatoes and vegetables. The buffet table and guest tables have been set, and the drinks are chilled. I have to make coffee and heat water for tea. We'll be ready when the guests arrive."

Grabbing water pitchers, she stepped to the sink, looking out the large window. The riders must've just returned, as the ranch hands were already removing the saddles. Off to the side, she spotted Koa standing next to Trace, talking to one of the guests.

The look on her son's face, so full of admiration for his father, caused doubt to germinate in her chest. No matter Koa's relationship with Wyatt or Virgil or any of the men at Whistle Rock, they couldn't take the place of his father.

She recalled a conversation between her and Trace when he received the petition for divorce. He'd been stunned, didn't have a clue why she wanted to leave him. When she'd told him about a friend accusing him of cheating, he'd adamantly denied the allegation.

I may not be the best husband or father, but I love you and Koa. I'd never cheat on you, Emma.

His plea for understanding had plagued her since the divorce. Whether he'd cheated or not, they had been divorced for years.

There was no going back for a do-over. And there was the fact Trace hadn't given any indication he wanted to reconcile. Their time together had come and gone. He'd moved on and so had she.

Him showing up now had more to do with building a relationship with Koa than any feelings he may still harbor for her. There was a good chance Trace had a girlfriend, fiancée, or wife somewhere else. Her heart thudded in her chest. Was it possible he'd fallen in love and remarried?

"Stop it." Emma whispered the words, angry at herself for even caring if Trace had a woman in his life. She'd been the one to push for divorce. If there were regrets, she had only herself to blame.

The sound of Nacho leaving the kitchen for the huge, fenced outdoor barbeque area caught her attention. Picking up one tray of marinating meat, she followed him, sliding through the gate. The space had been designed as a modified kitchen with large grills, warming trays, and a giant pizza oven. Fans drove the intense heat upward, where a partial roof protected the area while allowing the temperature to remain manageable.

Setting the tray down on a prep table, she returned to the kitchen three more times to carry out marinated chicken, skewers of vegetables, and foil wrapped potatoes.

"I'm going to set out the appetizers, Nacho."

Wiping a sleeve across his forehead, he nodded, never averting his attention from the grill. "Check the desserts one more time, but don't set them out yet."

"Will do." Dashing back to the kitchen, she'd started closing the door when Koa's voice stopped her.

"Mom!" Running toward her, he stopped inches away, breathing heavily. "Can I eat with the guests tonight?"

"You know that's not allowed. Since it's the last night, you can eat dessert with them."

"But Allie wants me there. She doesn't have anyone to talk to. Well, other than old people." He wrinkled his nose. "Can I ask Wyatt or Virgil?"

"Is your dad eating with the guests?"

"Nope. He said he'll be busy setting up activities."

Looking past Koa to the men setting up the bonfire, she smiled. "Tell you what. Ask Allie and her grandpa if she can eat with you in the kitchen. I'm sure Wyatt and Nacho will be fine with that."

"Okay." Whirling around, he ran toward the guest cabins.

"What's he so fired up about?" Nacho wiped his hands down the once white apron.

She explained, hoping he didn't make a pest of himself with Allie's grandfather. "I sure hope there are more kids around his age during the rest of the summer. Maybe I should be more aggressive at setting up activities with his school buddies. The problem is it might be difficult inviting his friends here."

"Because of the dude ranch guests?" Nacho blew out a breath while waving a hand in the air. "No different than having them here before the people start showing up. Invite them. It'll work out."

She wasn't as sure. "I'll think about it, Nacho. Thanks."

"We're all family here, Em. Nobody's gonna mind Koa having a couple buddies over. I need to get back to the grill." He nodded toward the cabins, where a few guests were making their way toward the main lodge.

"I'd better check on the buffet tables and put out ice for the drinks."

"Mom!" Koa ran toward them with Allie right behind him.

Shaking his head, Nacho turned toward the grill area. "That boy has just one speed."

"Mom. Allie's grandpa said she could eat with me."

"That's wonderful. How about helping me finish getting the dining room ready for dinner?"

Koa looked at Allie, whose eager nod told him how much she wanted to help.

"Great." This time, when Emma turned toward the kitchen, a white truck pulling into the ranch caught her attention.

She waited until Mack Devore got out, wondering if he'd come to see her or one of the Bonners. His eyes locked on her as his hand raised in greeting, and he began walking toward her. Emma glanced down at the children.

"Go on inside. You can add ice to the pitchers on the counter, then fill them with water."

"Who's that man, Mom?"

"A friend of the Bonners, Koa."

Brows lowering, his mouth twisted. "But why did he wave at you?"

"I've met him. Now get on inside and fill the pitchers." She held the door open for the two, Koa hesitating a few seconds before following Allie inside.

Letting out a relieved breath, Emma walked toward Mack. Until now, Koa hadn't been aware of her having dinner with the older rancher. He'd spent the night with a friend on the two occasions when they'd gone out. She dreaded answering the questions she knew would come from her much too precocious son.

"Hi, Emma."

"Mack."

"How are you?"

A smile tilted the corners of her mouth. "I'm doing fine. You look particularly handsome this evening. Going on a date?" Wincing, she wanted to call the question back. Then she noticed the faint red blush creep up his neck and onto his jaw.

He didn't answer her question. "There's a ranching association dinner tonight. They're held twice a year. Speakers, dinner...the usual."

"Sounds nice. Well, I'd better get inside. Tonight's the last dinner before the guests head out tomorrow." Turning away, she glanced over her shoulder before going inside. "Have a great time."

Mack watched her leave, not reaching out to stop her. Placing fisted hands on his hips, he stared at the ground, knowing he'd messed everything up.

"What brings you here, Mack?" Wyatt extended his hand. "You don't look so good."

Shaking hands, Mack blew out a frustrated breath. "I came by to ask Emma to dinner tomorrow, but she picked up on my clothes. Must've figured I was going on a date tonight."

"Are you?"

"In a sense. I'm going to the association dinner. I didn't want to go alone, so I invited Lydia to go with me."

"The owner of the bakery and coffee shop?"

"That's her. We've known each other for years, are good friends, but nothing more. I'm lousy at this kind of thing."

Chuckling, Wyatt placed a hand on Mack's shoulder and squeezed. "Give her a few days, then call and invite her to dinner. With guests turning over on Sundays, during the week is best. Tuesday or Wednesday." Wyatt thought about mentioning Trace, dismissing the idea. This was between Emma and Mack.

"You're right. You aren't going to the dinner, Wyatt?"

"Pop and Mom are going. You know how much he enjoys these shindigs. They already left. He doesn't want to miss anything."

"That's Anson, all right. This time, ranchers out of Jackson Hole are invited. Should be a good crowd. Well, I'd best get going. And I'll take your advice on Emma. She's a real sweetheart."

"Yes, she is."

Wyatt didn't move, watching Mack get into his truck. He'd known Mack's deceased wife, knew how much the rancher loved her. It had to be hard getting back into dating after over twenty-five years. The good news was Mack's two grown boys were still at home, helping to keep the rancher centered.

"Hey, boss." Trace came up next to him, brushing his hands down his jeans. "Everything is set up for tonight's campfire and entertainment. Any problem with me eating with the men?"

"Instead of with the guests?"

Trace watched the white truck drive out of the ranch, disappearing up the road. He'd seen the man talking to Emma, forcing himself to stay put and not make a fool of himself.

"Trace?"

"Uh, yes."

"I have no problem with it." Wyatt nodded toward the road. "That was Mack Devore. He's got a successful ranching operation north of here. Our ranches share a border. Good man."

"Yeah, I'm sure he is." He pulled his attention from the road to Wyatt. "Unless you have more for me, I'll go check with Barrel, see what's left to do before the guests finish dinner."

"Go ahead, Trace." His jaw tight, Wyatt wondered what would happen when the tensions between Trace, Emma, and possibly Mack, blew up. All good people. The first two valuable to Whistle Rock operations. A sense of foreboding washed over him as he walked toward the barn. A foreboding he was powerless to erase.

Chapter Nine

The last evening exceeded expectations. When the cowboy entertainment ended, guests danced to a local band, laughing, and carrying on until after eleven. Even Nacho and Emma left their aprons behind to join in the festivities.

Trace's attention shifted between her and the female guests asking for a dance. He accommodated each one, pleased with the joy he saw on their faces. Unlike the rodeo circuit, the women weren't looking for anything more than a wonderful time on their last night at Whistle Rock Ranch.

Walking a group of older women back to their cabins, he accepted hugs, encouraging them to come back again. Most told him they were already planning a return trip.

Heading back to the campfire and dwindling crowd, he spotted Koa, Allie, and her grandfather walking toward the guest cabins. The children had draped their arms over each other's shoulders, talking and laughing as they walked. Their camaraderie brought a lump to Trace's throat.

Glancing around, he searched for Emma. She stood off to one side, talking to Wyatt's wife, Daisy, and Virgil's wife, Lily. Fading into the background, he continued watching the three women. All were animated, laughing one minute, growing serious the next. He wished he had the right to join them, take Emma's hand in his, and walk her to their shared cabin.

Reality was much different. She'd be returning to the apartment she shared with Koa in the main lodge, and he'd retreat to his bed in the bunkhouse. The future hadn't turned out as he'd envisioned when they'd walked down the aisle at their wedding.

Emma had been the most beautiful woman he'd ever seen. All these years later, no other woman could compare.

Trace waited in the darkness, unwilling to leave before Emma returned to her apartment. He'd already spotted Koa enter the back of the lodge.

Little time passed before the three women decided to head to their own beds. Watching her enter the lodge, he pushed away from the side of the barn. The two people he loved most were safe, and would soon be in deep sleep. He meant to be right behind them.

Jonah Bonner, the second oldest son, sat in the small family dining room, chowing down on a simple lunch of beef sandwiches and salad. Wyatt, Gage, their parents, Anson and Margie, plus Jasper and Virgil, completed the group.

They'd found the best time to review the previous week was right after church on Sundays, a few hours before the new batch of guests arrived. The agenda for the meeting focused on whether or not to extend the dude ranch calendar by one week.

"We have a few openings until the middle of September." Jonah scanned the list of reservations. "We're full this coming week and the next. There are two openings the following week, and about the same until our projected closing date in the fall."

Anson glanced up from the paper in his hand. "Remind me of the existing date."

"The end of September, Pop," Jonah answered. "Canvassing other ranches in Wyoming, about fifty percent stay open until the end of October, and a few until the end of November. Two or three are open all year."

Wyatt looked at his younger brother, the business and finance whiz. "What do you recommend, Jonah?"

"Extend until the end of October."

Virgil drummed fingers on the table while absorbing Jonah's recommendation. "Do you want to increase the number of guests per week?"

"Not this year. We decided to allow up to twenty-four guests each week for the first season. I believe we should consider increasing this to forty guests next season. It would require building a few more cabins, which could start within the next couple weeks."

Wyatt made a few notes before looking at Jonah. "Do we have time to advertise a longer season? As I recall, we need a minimum of sixteen guests to break even."

Jonah looked at his mother, who handled much of the marketing and publicity. "Mom, what do you think?"

"It could be tough. The other ranches have been advertising their longer season since last winter. We'd be coming in late. Do we have any idea the capacity the other ranches are experiencing for October?"

Jonah shook his head. "I haven't had a chance to check."

"I'll call around. I know many of the ranchers, and if I don't, Anson does. Right, honey?" Margie looked at her husband. He still struggled with having so many greenhorns on the ranch.

"I don't know if they'll give me the numbers, but I can try."

"Is that something you can get to within the next couple days, Pop?"

"Not much else on my calendar, Jonah."

Soft chuckles rolled around the table. Since Anson handed the reins of Whistle Rock Ranch to Wyatt, he'd been finding it hard to back off and let his son make the tough choices. This reality was one of the reasons he and Margie had vacationed so much over the last few months. Anson couldn't interfere while being thousands of miles away.

Wyatt tapped his pen on the table before glancing around the table. "We have to keep in mind this is a working cattle ranch and horse breeding facility. That's where the big money is for us. We're already short men. Lengthening the season won't hurt too much, but we need to plan for it. Same with adding cabins and capacity. We've got three operations going on and can't afford for any to lose momentum."

"How many men are we short?" Anson's mouth twisted into a scowl.

"Eight to ten over the spring, summer, and early fall. It's tough to keep them on throughout the winter. The best situation would be to hire men with ranching experience, including cattle and horse breeding. They can move between those activities and the dude ranch when it's running."

Jonah ran a few numbers, grimacing before meeting Wyatt's expectant gaze. "So we're talking a temporary increase for about seven or eight months?"

"That's what I'm thinking."

Jonah ran a few more numbers. "Can you get by with five?"

Rubbing the back of his neck, he tilted the chair to look out the window. "Virgil and I can make it work."

"Let's talk about this more, Wyatt. I have some ideas."

"You can talk about it now, Virgil," Anson said.

"Not yet. I need to think about this more." Everyone around the table knew this was Virgil's way of giving a warning. He wasn't ready. Since a young boy, he'd required time to think through an issue, and would only talk about it when he had something useful to say.

Jonah finished writing the last of his notes and looked up. "Pop's going to check with other dude ranches about their schedules. When he has the information, we can discuss lengthening this year, and next year's calendar.

Wyatt and Virgil will discuss the number of new hires and let me know the results. That's all I have. Anyone else have something we need to discuss?"

A few shook their heads, while others stood up to leave, signaling the end of their meeting.

Virgil placed a hand on Wyatt's shoulder. "Let's go outside and talk."

They walked to the newest barn, which held the family's horses, stopping at the back. Leaning against the empty stall, Virgil scratched his stubble.

"Trace knows a lot of people from his rodeo days. He mentioned to Barrel that there are others like him who are ready to get out. We could get by with four men to work with the guests and free up our regular guys to focus on breeding and the cattle."

"Could work. What would the four do when the dude ranch is closed?"

"If Trace can find guys with good ranching experience, we might be able to keep them on over the winter. It'll all depend on their skills."

Wyatt hooked his thumbs in his jeans, looking down at his boots. "Has Emma said anything to you?"

"About Trace?"

"Yeah. Neither one has said a word to me."

"That's good news, Wyatt. Maybe they've come to an understanding. Koa seems to stick to Trace like a thistle to Trooper's coat." Virgil picked up an old horseshoe, passing it from one hand to the other. "Do you want me to talk to Trace about more men? I'm certain he'll help."

"Go ahead. I'll put the word out we're looking for men who have ranching experience. A background in horse breeding would be a big plus."

"You're hoping to keep them on all year?"

"If we can. It takes a lot of time to hire good men."

"Took months to find someone with Trace's background. Several guests took the time to tell me how much they loved him." Virgil chuckled. "A group of five older women came to me last night to express how much they enjoyed him. They had a great time all around, but Trace took the time to talk to them. They're already looking at dates for next year."

"We could use four more like him."

"Dreaming is good, white man."

Wyatt threw back his head and laughed, turned away and walked out of the barn.

Chapter Ten

"Everything is finished and in the large refrigerator." Emma ran both hands down her apron. "There's plenty for the twenty-four guests arriving late this afternoon."

Nacho acknowledged her with a grunt, his attention focused on several breakfast casseroles for Monday morning. "Why don't you take the rest of the day off? Take Koa to town."

Removing the soiled apron, she tossed it into a laundry bin. "Maybe I will. Assuming I can pry him away from Trace."

"That boy of yours is starving for his daddy's attention." Covering the glass baking dishes with plastic wrap, he slid them into the refrigerator below the appetizers Emma had prepared.

The first night meal included heavy hors d'oeuvres, fresh bread and cheese platters, and dessert, with coffee, tea, juice, or water. They'd tried a full dinner for the first group of guests in early summer. Most of the food had gone uneaten. The second group had been offered the appetizers and desserts. Not a crumb was left when the guests returned to their cabins.

Leaning against the counter, Emma crossed her arms. "He's a clone of Trace. Even before the divorce, Koa followed his father around."

"That bothered you?"

"Not at all. It upset my mother. She hated the way her grandson worshiped his father. She has a real dislike for cowboys, rodeo cowboys in particular. Guess it doesn't matter any longer."

Pushing away from the counter, she startled at the knock on the kitchen's back door. Employees didn't knock, as the kitchen remained open for those who worked at Whistle Rock, meaning the person outside may have ended up at the wrong door.

Opening it, she was surprised to see Mack.

"Hello, Emma. Hope it's all right to stop by."

"Of course it is. Are you here to see Anson or Margie?" Pulling the door wide, she moved aside so he could walk past her.

"I'm here to see you." He shot a look at Nacho, who took the hint.

"I have to get some items for breakfast tomorrow, Emma. Be back in a minute."

She knew it wasn't the truth, but didn't argue. "Would you like some coffee, Mack?"

"I've had plenty, thanks. I stopped by to invite you to dinner."

Closing the door, she glanced outside to see Trace and Koa near the barn. Emma hoped they hadn't seen Mack. "Tonight?"

"If you don't have other plans."

Looking down at the worn jeans and blouse, she debated what to do. "I should clean up."

"You look great."

"Can we go somewhere casual? As in very casual?"

"Wherever you want to go."

Clasping her hands together, she pursed her lips. Emma felt conflicted. Mack had taken another woman to the local cattle association dinner the night before. It truly didn't bother her much. Still, it seemed odd for a stable, mature man such as Mack to go out with two different women on subsequent nights. She thought of Mack as a friend, doubting their occasional dinners would ever turn into something more.

Emma knew if she remarried, she'd want more children. Mack had made it clear he was finished with that part of his life. His two boys were in their twenties, with plans to someday marry and have children of their own. Grandchildren were perfect for this stage of Mack's life.

"Give me ten minutes and I'll be ready." The first thing she'd do was leave a note for Koa, letting him know she had to go to town and would be home soon.

A slow smile appeared on Mack's face. "Take as long as you need. Is there a bottle of water around here?"

Opening the second refrigerator, she pulled out a bottle. "Would you prefer a glass?"

Taking it from her hand, he removed the cap. "The bottle is fine. Thanks."

Trace watched from a distance as the truck Emma was in left the ranch, taking the highway to town. He recognized the driver as an older rancher Virgil had introduced him to a few days earlier. A widower with a successful operation down the road from Whistle Rock. He found himself wondering if Virgil knew the man had set his sights on Emma.

The thought of another man spending time with her turned his stomach. Trace had been so focused on getting his family back, he hadn't considered her having feelings for someone else.

He looked toward the door leading into the apartment where Emma and Koa lived. Did his son know about Mack Devore? Trace doubted it.

The appearance of the rancher added another complication to an already difficult situation. He'd never run from a challenge in his life, and he wouldn't fall into that trap now. He knew getting his family back was a long shot.

His closest friend called him a fool, told him to move on with his life. But Jake had never been married, didn't have a kid.

Trace couldn't do it. Couldn't walk away now that he'd found them.

Reaching into a back pocket, he pulled out his harmonica, turning it over in his hand. Emma had given it to him on their first Christmas together.

She'd remembered a story he'd told about his father playing. Trace had always wanted a harmonica so he could play with his father. He'd asked for one Christmas after Christmas, but it never materialized.

He smiled at the memory, bringing the instrument to his mouth. The slow song fit his mood. Nostalgic and melancholy, the volume low so as not to attract attention. Emma had always loved the song. Whenever in a gloomy mood, he'd play it to help him recall better times.

When finished, he wiped it on his sleeve and stared down at the mouth harp before sliding it into a pocket. Striding to the bunkhouse, he didn't hear or feel the grumbling in his stomach. All he could think about was Emma and the man she rode away with.

"So you want me to contact some of my rodeo friends to see if any are ready to try something else?" Trace tipped the chair back, stared at the ceiling a moment before lowering his gaze to Virgil. His boss had entered the bunkhouse early the next morning, wanting a meeting before Trace began working with the new roster of guests. "Yeah, I can do that. You said Wyatt is going to put the word out around here?"

"And to a few other ranchers who may have more men than they need."

"Can I tell them if all works out, they could be offered a job all year round?"

Virgil nodded. "As long as you don't guarantee them anything. We need to assess their skills, make sure they fit around here."

"When would you want them to start?"

"If they're available now, fine. If not until spring, that's fine too. We'll assess each man individually."

A slow smile spread across Trace's face. "Any objection to hiring a woman?"

Rubbing his stubbled jaw, Virgil grinned. "Not if they can do the job, and have no issue staying in the bunkhouse with the men."

"The woman I'm thinking of wouldn't have a problem sharing. Anything else?" Trace started to stand, stilling when Virgil waved him back down.

"How are you and Emma getting along?"

The question startled Trace. "Good."

"I ask out of concern for Emma. We can't afford to lose her." Virgil tapped a pen on a pad of paper. "To be honest, when we figured out who you were, Wyatt and I made the decision not to say anything to you or Emma. We believed it was none of our business. Your relationship still isn't, but things have changed. You're both valuable to the ranch."

Trace felt his shoulders sag in relief. "Thanks, Virgil."

"As long as you and Emma get along, there'll be no issues." Pressing his hands on top of the desk, he stood.

"Let me or Wyatt know if one of your friends is interested in working for us."

"I'll get right on it."

Jasper sat in the shade of the lodge's porch, watching Trace explain the day's activities to the new crop of guests. He'd given them a small taste of his background, enough to let them know he understood ranching and rodeo.

"Are you feeling all right?" Monica Redstar, the estranged wife who'd been absent from his and Virgil's lives for years, sat down in the chair next to him.

"Tired is all." Jasper suffered from late onset adult asthma. "I'll be fine in a few minutes." He reached out, taking her hand in his.

They'd been dancing around what to do with their vague relationship since she arrived at Whistle Rock Ranch. Most thought they'd divorced years ago. Even Anson and Margie believed their good friends had ended their marriage. They hadn't.

Squeezing his hand, Monica rubbed her thumb across his palm. "Don't push yourself, sweetheart. No one expects you to work every day. Maybe we should do what we discussed and get away for a while."

He lifted a brow. "A vacation?"

"Well, yes."

"What would people think of us going away together? Most believe we're divorced."

Monica laughed at Jasper's obvious attempt at parroting her concerns. She'd said the same to him a few weeks earlier when he mentioned going on an extended trip.

"We should renew our vows." He'd mentioned this several times since her return.

She'd been hesitant to take the step. It would mean moving into his apartment on the ranch, giving up the independence she cherished, risking another broken heart. Both knew it was Jasper who'd driven her away, kept her and Virgil apart. Monica knew she'd never completely forgiven him for the pain he'd caused.

"I'm not ready, Jasper."

"It's been months. I've apologized many times. There's nothing more I can do." The finality in his voice twisted her stomach.

He was right. She'd been wavering since he'd first mentioned they live together. Monica had objected, saying they should renew their vows first. When he'd agreed, she'd still hesitated.

"All right. I will think about it and we'll talk again." Standing, she bent to kiss his cheek.

"Soon, Monica. This must be settled."

Throat tight, she entered the lodge before the tears at the back of her eyes fell.

Chapter Eleven

Emma set down the knife used for slicing fruit, wiped damp hands on her apron before grabbing her ringing phone. Seeing the name, she winced. Her mother, Pauline, had called twice the night before, when Emma was having dinner with Mack. She hadn't called her back.

Sliding the phone away, she continued slicing fruit for the large salad the guests would have at lunch. Nacho prepared seasoned hamburger patties, setting them in a tray alongside stacks of bratwurst and hotdogs. He'd soon head out to the grill while Emma put out corn chips, guacamole, and salsa.

This group of guests was different from last week's. While they were older, many in their sixties, the current group were in their thirties and forties, a few in their twenties. Several with children Koa's age or younger.

Emma hadn't seen her son since he'd rushed away from his breakfast to join Trace on a two hour trail ride with the guests. They'd spend an hour before dismounting to take a short hike along a stream. Barrel would point out different plants and give a brief summary of the area's history before handing out snacks. They'd take a different route back to the ranch. A little easier and shorter, the group would arrive an hour before lunch.

She glanced up at the wall clock. Eleven o'clock, meaning the horses should come into view soon. Before returning to their cabins to freshen up, the guests would be given an updated schedule with any changes.

Monday afternoons always included a photography class presented by Daisy, a calf roping demonstration by the ranch hands, and guests learning how to handle a lariat. Three calves created from wood were placed in the largest corral. The last was a favorite of the younger men and children. A few guests would opt to walk around, read, or nap before wine and cheese, or cookies and milk, were set out in the lodge.

Hearing voices, she spotted the riders dismounting outside the barn. Less than a minute later, Koa came rushing into the kitchen, sucking in air.

"We saw another dead calf, Mom. Dad kept everyone back, but a few saw it." Chuckling, he reached out, snagging a chip. "One lady threw up."

"Koa, no making fun of the guests."

"Dad and Barrel told her to stay back, but she rode past them. Her own fault, Mom."

Maybe it was, but Emma knew how one negative experience could ruin the week for a guest. Before she could say anything else, the door opened. Trace stood in the opening, whipping off his hat when he saw Emma.

"Is there some Sprite I can give to one of the guests?"

"Bet it's for the woman who lost her breakfast. Right, Dad?"

Trace's stern expression and raised brow silenced his son. "I wouldn't ask, but it could help."

Emma walked to one of the two refrigerators, removing a can of Sprite. "Does she want a glass and ice?"

"No. Actually, one that isn't chilled might be better."

"Ah, right."

"I'll get it, Mom." Koa rushed around a corner, returning with a can at room temperature.

"Thanks, son." Nodding at Emma, he placed the hat back on his head, closing the door behind him.

Koa noticed his mother staring after his father. "You aren't yelling at him."

The comment caused her to tear her attention from Trace. "I never yelled at him."

"All the time. You and Grandma. I remember 'cause I'd run to my room and cover my ears." Snagging another chip, he rushed outside to follow Trace.

Stunned, Emma thought back on the months prior to the divorce, something she typically tried to avoid. She recalled arguing, accusing Trace of cheating. Did she raise her voice, yell? Emma couldn't recall.

She did remember Trace denying the allegations. He never raised his voice in anger. Sometimes, he'd shout while competing, or yell at someone who acted in a way which put others in danger. Not once in their years together did he raise his voice at her.

The image which caused the most hurt, made her wonder if her accusations had been correct, was his face. Trace's features fell as he shook his head. He'd denied any involvement with another woman, been hurt she'd even suggested he'd betray her.

Back then, she'd been young, vulnerable, angry at his long absences after Koa's birth. Emma knew what marrying a rodeo star included, yet she'd thrown everything back at him when a friend had told her of his activities.

Recalling that period of time, she had to admit the friend was more an acquaintance. They'd never met for lunch or coffee, never spoken on the phone. Their few encounters had been at the rodeo grounds during competitions. Could she have been wrong in believing what the woman had to say about Trace?

What truly stuck in her head was how her mother grasped onto the charges, pushed Emma to get a divorce. Had she allowed her mother to poison her thoughts?

"How are you doing in here?" Nacho walked in from outside, scanned the food laid out on the preparation counter.

Still stuck in memories of the past, she blew out a shaky breath. "Fine. Ready to take everything out to the buffet table." She could feel his intense gaze on her, fought the urge to squirm.

"Do you need help?"

"No. I've got this, Nacho. Go ahead and concentrate on the grill."

"The guests will be arriving in about fifteen minutes."

Emma didn't move, her mind still whirling with doubt about the breakup of her marriage. Even if she'd been wrong about Trace, did it still matter after five years?

Stepping to the window, she stared outside at a group of people talking. A woman turned toward her, causing Emma's breath to catch. An image from the past floated across her mind. Her chest squeezed.

"It couldn't be," she whispered. The woman had the same bleached blonde, frizzy hair. The height and weight were about the same, as were the generous curves. She held the hand of a tall, muscled man Emma knew she'd never seen before.

"Mom. Dad wants to know if it's all right for me to sit with him at lunch. Can I?"

Continuing to stare, her heart persisted its painful beat. "Mom!"

Emma startled at her son's voice. "What?"

"I asked if it was okay for me to eat with Dad at lunch."

Rubbing a temple, she tried to refocus, pull her mind from the woman outside. "Is he eating with the guests?"

"Yes. He says it's okay with him."

"I suppose it wouldn't be a problem. You need to check with Nacho."

"Already did. He says he doesn't care and it's up to you. Please, Mom."

Taking a quick look outside, she saw the woman still with the others. Still held the man's hand.

"Fine. Mind your manners."

"I will. Thanks!"

She heard the outside door close as she continued to watch the woman. There wasn't anything she could do right now. The guests would be coming in any minute, and the food still needed to be placed on the buffet table.

Hurrying, she moved with practiced speed between the kitchen and dining area. The buns, condiments, plates, silverware, chips and dips, plus drinks were in their usual places. The fruit salad came out next, followed by covered dishes filled with baked beans, potato salad, and coleslaw.

The desserts would normally be brought out while the guests ate lunch. Today, she decided to place platters of cookies, brownies, lemon squares, berry tarts, and pecan pie now. Until she verified the woman was who she believed, Emma didn't want to be spotted.

Voices on the front porch alerted her to the guests arriving. Dashing back to the kitchen, she looked through the sliver of glass. The woman entered soon after the door opened, heading straight for the drink table.

Emma continued to watch, wanting to be certain before she approached the woman. When Trace entered, her uncertainty faded away. Spotting the woman, he walked to her, setting a hand on her shoulder. After a moment, he shook the hand of the man beside her. The three acted as if they knew each other.

Feeling lightheaded, Emma moved away from the door, trying to make sense of what she'd seen. She didn't believe in coincidences, but what else could this be?

Trace had been at the ranch a little over a week, and all the slots were full through the beginning of September. He wouldn't have known about any of the guests who'd already booked space.

Emma reminded herself she'd never told Trace the name of the woman who'd accused him of cheating. He'd never asked.

Turning away, she worked to formulate a plan. When Nacho entered with a large platter of cooked meat, she relaxed. Holding out her hands, she took the platter from him.

"I'll cook the rest, but we don't want to hold them up from eating."

"No problem. I'll get this right out."

Taking a deep breath to fortify herself, she straightened, lifting her chin. Entering the dining room, she set the platter down, turning to face Trace. When he saw her, his smile widened. Motioning her to join them, she didn't hesitate.

"Emma, you remember Blossom McGuire from the rodeo, right?"

Blossom's eyes widened at the same time Emma offered a frigid smile. "Of course I do. I trust you've had a happy life since we last spoke."

"I, um...yes. Life has been good, Emma." Blossom's gaze darted to the man beside her. "Do you remember Brent?"

"Vaguely." Emma held out her hand. "I hope you're enjoying your stay."

Gently shaking her hand, he put his arm around Blossom's waist. "It's great. I didn't know what to expect. We've both been impressed with what we've seen so far."

"So, you and Trace work here?"

"We do. Who would've thought, right, Blossom?"

"Um, yes."

"Mom. Dad." Koa stopped between them. "Can I sit with the table of kids?"

Trace looked at Emma, lifting a brow. When she nodded, he set a hand on Koa's head. "Best manners, right?"

"Sure, Dad. Thanks."

"And no running in the dining room."

"Right." Smiling, Koa took off as fast as he'd arrived.

"Looks just like you, Trace." Brent tightened his hold around Blossom's waist. "We hope to have kids someday."

Glancing at Blossom's left hand, she noticed the pair of rings. "I'd better get back to the kitchen. Enjoy your meal." Sending Blossom a meaningful look, Emma retreated to the safety of her job.

The door opened several minutes later as Trace walked in. Stopping within a few feet of her, he rested his hands on his hips.

"Do you want to tell me what just happened in there?"

"Not really."

"So I wasn't imagining something going on between you and Blossom."

Looking at the ground, she shook her head. "No."

Sucking in a slow breath, he watched her discomfort grow. "She said you two haven't spoken in at least five years."

Licking her lips, she again shook her head. "No, we haven't."

"The timing is interesting, don't you think?"

She didn't respond.

"We're going to need to talk, Emma."

"What for?"

"Because we have unsettled issues between us."

"It is settled. We're divorced and I have custody of Koa."

"I'm sure that works fine for you, but from my perspective, it isn't all right with me or Koa."

"Koa is doing fine."

Scrubbing a hand down his face, Trace stared at her. "You need to ask him how he feels, Em. Look, I need to get back to the table. All I'm asking is for us to sit down and talk. You must decide if this is too much to ask."

Chapter Twelve

It wasn't too much to ask, Emma thought as she stared at the ceiling near midnight.

Trace hadn't asked for anything over the last five years. Other than an occasional call and gifts at Christmas and Koa's birthday, he'd left them alone. She didn't need to speak with her son to know he missed his father. The way he followed Trace around broke her heart.

She knew now the mistakes made when throwing away her marriage. The decision had been impulsive, predicated on what she suspected might be bad information meant to stoke her anger.

"I never should've listened to Blossom or my mother," she whispered in the darkened bedroom.

Working and living at Whistle Rock Ranch had given her time to think through what she'd done. Trace showing up had emphasized the mistakes she'd made, the broken promise to him. Five years ago, he'd asked for time alone to sort out what had really happened. She'd refused, telling him she already knew the truth. It pained her to recall how she'd treated him.

No, it wasn't too much to ask for a conversation between the two of them.

Trace couldn't sleep. He'd left the bunkhouse an hour earlier, heading to the barn and his horse. It's what he'd done since a boy when facing what he considered insurmountable problems. A math test or essay were big issues back then. His troubles as an adult were so much worse, and unlike when a child, impacted people other than himself.

He'd been hard on Emma tonight. Much harder than he'd intended, given how long he'd been at the ranch. Trace had planned to wait for a month, maybe six weeks, before requesting they talk. Blossom's appearance had changed his thinking.

The woman had set something off in Emma. He'd never seen her so inhospitable. The fact her hostile attitude had been directed at a paying guest made it that much worse.

Trace had seated himself next to Blossom and her husband, Brent, during dinner. Neither had commented on Emma's uncharacteristic coolness. He wondered what had caused the animosity she directed at Blossom.

Tomorrow would be another full day of activities. He'd be joining Gage Bonner to take twenty of the guests on a hike to hidden caves. At the opposite end of the cave was a waterfall. They'd eat lunch at the fall before returning to base camp. Koa would be joining them, as would several children around his age.

This trip took most of the day. The group would arrive back at the ranch close to three, just in time for afternoon refreshments.

Impatience pushed him to speak with Emma after the snacks, but instinct told him to give her a few days. Maybe she'd approach him.

"You're up late." Jimmy French, a tall, lanky ranch hand with messy blond hair and striking green eyes walked toward him. Guileless and hardworking, everyone liked the young cowhand.

"Couldn't sleep. What's got you coming to the barn so late?"

"Same." Jimmy placed his back against the barn's siding.

"What's causing your lack of sleep?"

"Girlfriend troubles. She's decided I'll never have enough money to support us, buy a house, and raise a family. The thing is, she's probably right."

Trace knew a lot of guys on the rodeo circuit who faced the same dilemma. Traveling all over the country added another problem to keeping a relationship.

"Maybe you haven't found the right girl."

"That's what Barrel says. He keeps telling me the right girl won't be so negative about my prospects. I'm beginning to believe he's right."

"Maybe you should listen to Barrel."

"Yeah, maybe I should. What about you?"

Trace's brow rose. "What about me?"

"Why can't you sleep?"

"A lot on my mind, Jimmy."

"Is Koa really your son?"

The corners of his mouth turned upward. "He is."

"Great kid."

"Yeah, he is. His mother has done a good job raising him."

"Gotta be hard. Not being in your son's life. Guess that's why you're here."

Trace rubbed his jaw while staring at the main lodge. He was here for both Koa and Emma. "How long have you been working here?"

"A while now. About two years or so. The Bonners are good people. So is Virgil and his family, including his wife, Lily. She's a real sweet lady. Works at the hospital. Guess I'll head inside. See you in the morning."

Trace stayed a few minutes longer. Pulling out his phone, he checked the time. Too late for a call, but a text would work just as well. Tapping his message, he ended with *Love you*, then touched Send.

"Doctor Worrel checked the cattle, but didn't find enough evidence to vaccinate the entire herd." Wyatt stared out at the western pastures. "I spoke with the guests who saw the dead animal. They're doing fine and understand it's a disease which can't be passed onto humans. We gave them gift certificates to the shop, which most said wasn't necessary."

Virgil followed Wyatt's gaze, seeing nothing except the western horizon. "We should send out riders each morning to precheck areas where we're taking guests."

"Good idea. Arrange it with Barrel. Has Trace gotten back to you about possible new ranch hands?"

Virgil opened his mouth to respond, closing when Trace joined, his phone to his ear.

"Hold on, Sam." He looked at Wyatt, then Virgil. "I have someone interested in working here. Grew up on a ranch, excellent with horses, worked in rodeo crew for a few years, and is ready for a change. Is there time this week to interview?"

"Anytime in the afternoon. After the afternoon activities. Virgil and I can interview him together to save time."

"Sam—"

"I heard them. Tomorrow afternoon?"

"Great. See you then, Sam." Ending the call, he slid it in a pocket. "Tomorrow afternoon. I haven't heard back from the others. I'll let you know when they call. I'd better get back to the stable. We've got a ride going out soon." Shooting a look at the kitchen's back door, his jaw tightened as he strode toward the already saddled horses.

Placing the last of the afternoon snacks away, Emma wiped down the counter, slowing at the laughter and cheers of the guests outside. Turning toward the window, she saw a group of men and women clustered around the corral used for demonstrations. Scattered among them were the children, including Koa. She could just make out a rope twirling in the air.

Emma didn't often revisit her time in high school. She'd been on the rodeo team as a barrel racer. Doing well enough to try out for the college team, she competed for two years before her mother's health deteriorated, and she dropped out. Her mouth twisted at the bitter taste.

Within a month of Emma's return, her mother rallied without ever divulging what ailed her. It was during her time home Emma met and fell in love with Trace during a break in his rodeo schedule. It wasn't long before she was pregnant with Koa.

Leaning against the kitchen workstation, she continued to watch the guests. For about the hundredth time, she wondered if offering a demonstration of barrel racing would be a good addition to the list of activities.

She'd never worked up the courage to ask Wyatt or Virgil, partly because barrel racing was years in her past. Emma estimated as much as twelve years, a long time to be out of the saddle.

"We're having King Ranch enchiladas and street tacos tonight, Emma. We'll need three salads."

Turning to face Nacho, she smiled. "Green, fruit, and macaroni with your special sauce, which I've already made.

The flan and churros are ready, as are assorted Mexican cookies and pastries. There will also be plenty of vanilla and chocolate ice cream."

"With caramel, chocolate, and fudge sauces?"

"Of course. Why don't you go lay down for a while, Nacho? I'll double check everything and make certain nothing is missed."

Scrubbing a hand over his face, he offered a weary smile. "Maybe I will. It's been a long day."

"How about I make you a cup of Mexican hot chocolate?"

"You don't have time, Emma."

"I'll make time. Go on. I'll bring it to you."

Watching him leave on shaky legs, she was reminded of the numerous times he winces in pain while rubbing his lower back. Emma believed he'd work until his body gave out.

Using Nacho's family recipe, she fixed the Mexican chocolate, placing a dollop of whipped cream on top. He'd made it for Koa many times, explaining each step so the young boy could fix it for his mother. To her surprise, he'd brought a huge cup to her the last Mother's Day. Best hot chocolate she'd ever tasted.

"Mom, Dad asked me to let you know the activities are over."

She found it interesting Trace had sent the message rather than Virgil or Wyatt. "Thanks, honey."

Perching himself on a stool, he leaned on the counter, searching for something to eat. "What are we having?"

"Enchiladas and tacos."

"Chicken or beef?"

"Both, Koa. The same as every week."

Jumping down from the stool, he hurried to the refrigerator. Spying the ramekins filled with flan, he reached for one.

"Don't even think about it."

"Ah, Mom. I'm starving."

"You know the rules. The guests eat their meals first, then you can have one."

"If there are any left." He mimicked her tone, making Emma laugh.

"Have you made any friends?"

Mouth twisting, he shook his head. "They all brought friends with them. Last week was better with Allie here. When are the Bakers coming back?"

Koa had become friends with ranch hand Owen Baker's son, Cory, and daughter, Janie. Plus, Emma and Marta Baker had formed a friendship.

"This weekend. You'll have plenty of friends to play with once they return."

"Yeah, but what do I do now?"

"Why don't you invite one of your school friends to the ranch? They could spend the night and do the activities with you."

"That'd be great." Running to her, he held out his hand.

"I'll call the mother, Koa. Tell me who you want to invite."

"Ryan Olsen."

Dragging her phone from a pocket, she began to scroll her contacts, stopping when it rang.

"Ignore it, Mom."

Emma wanted to. Unfortunately, she couldn't ignore this call.

"It's Grandma."

"Ugh. Call her back."

"We'll see." Touching the Answer button, she braced herself for whatever ailed her mother today. "Hey, Mom. How are you?"

"Great, Emma. I have big news."

"What's that?"

"You aren't going to believe it. I'm on my way to Whistle Rock Ranch."

Chapter Thirteen

Closing her eyes, Emma searched for the right words to respond. It wasn't that she didn't love her mother. She did.

Emma just couldn't live close to her any longer. The negative attitude, her constant complaints about everything, created a terrible environment for raising Koa.

"Are you already on your way?" Perhaps she could still talk her out of traveling.

"I am. Friends are staying in Brilliance with relatives for a month and offered to drive me both ways."

Lowering the phone, Emma groaned. "Koa, why don't you head outside while I talk to Grandma?"

He sent his mother a grin. "Okay."

She raised the phone back to her ear. "I'll need to find you a motel room in town."

"No, no. I'd rather stay at the ranch."

"There are no open cabins or rooms. We're right in the middle of the dude ranch season, Mother. With summer tourist season, there may not be any motel rooms for you. I wish you would've called me before leaving home."

"All I need is a bed, Emma. Surely you can find something at the ranch."

"I'm sorry, but there's nothing here. I'll call around and see what can be arranged in town. You'll need a rental car to get around. If you remember our conversation a couple weeks ago, I mentioned having no free time until late September. It's just not a good time, but I'll do what I can to find a place for you to stay."

"At the ranch?"

"In town, Mother." Closing her eyes, she pressed fingers against her right temple.

"Well," her mother huffed. "I never would've come if I knew I'd have to stay in town."

"I'm sorry about the timing. Maybe it would be best for you to take a bus home, and we'll plan for you to visit in a few months." Crossing her fingers, Emma held the phone to her ear, waiting for the answer. A full minute passed before her mother responded.

Blowing out what Emma knew was a long-suffering breath, her voice took on a whiney tone. "I suppose I can stay in town a week, then take a bus home."

Emma reminded herself a week in town was a great deal better than four weeks on the ranch. "I'll start calling around. When will you arrive in Brilliance?"

"Late tonight."

"I'd better find you a motel. I'll call as soon as I make reservations. Love you, Mother."

"Yes, yes."

Emma stared at the phone, surprised at the abrupt way the call ended. Choosing not to dwell on her mother's odd behavior, she made a call to the only motel she could recall.

"Hello, Helen. It's Emma out at Whistle Rock Ranch. How are you? Yeah, I'm fine too. My mother's coming into town tonight. Any chance you have a room for one week? She can move around, if needed. I'll take it. Do you need my card to hold it? Appreciate it. Her name is Pauline Bullard. I owe you, Helen. Thanks."

The call to her mother was quick, long enough to provide the name and address of the hotel. Hanging up, Emma felt a short-lived sense of relief.

Her mother would drive out to the ranch tomorrow, visit with Emma and Koa, and possibly learn Trace worked at Whistle Rock. Any hint of a peaceful visit would evaporate.

Trace stepped into a crisp morning, knowing the day would shift to warm, then hot by noon. Settling his hat on still damp hair from a quick shower, he headed to the stables.

It would be another busy day. All of them were during dude ranch season.

He thought of his own ranch in northern Wyoming. Trace had put in hours of hard work, along with a hefty chunk of his rodeo winnings, to make it a success. The risk had been worth the reward.

Much of the success was due to the expertise and connections of longtime rodeo man, Augustus Pride.

Without Augie, the venture never would've turned a profit so soon.

They were now evaluating the merits of buying an existing rodeo stock company located about twenty minutes from his ranch. The purchase would double their size while requiring a good deal more capital. If the sale went forward, it would mean he'd leave Whistle Rock Ranch sooner than intended.

"Morning, Trace." Jimmy French joined him as they entered the barn. "Cattle drive today."

"Yep. Most of the guests are going. The youngest ones will be staying behind for a painting class with Daisy and cooking class with Emma. Those on the drive will be eating lunch on the trail."

"They're going to crash once you return. It always happens on the cattle drive days."

"Good to know. This is a younger crowd than last week. Maybe they'll bounce back quicker."

Jimmy shrugged. "We can hope."

They busied themselves collecting tack, and selecting horses for each guest. By the time they were finished, they could hear the sounds of guests talking on the way to the main lodge for breakfast.

"You ready to eat, Jimmy?"

"I'm always ready. Let's grab breakfast."

"You go on. I need to make a call." Waiting until Jimmy was out of earshot, Trace tapped a speed dial number. "How's everything going?"

Emma got the call as the last guests left the lodge after breakfast. "Hello, Mother. How did you sleep?"

Pauline Bullard let out a long suffering sigh. "My back is stiff from the too soft mattress, and whoever was in the room next door yelled much of the night. Did you know the rooms are smaller than my closet at home?"

"No, Mother, I didn't. What do you have planned for today?"

"Driving to the ranch, of course. I thought we could spend the day together."

Pinching the bridge of her nose, Emma was glad her mother couldn't see her frustration. "Today won't work, as I'm too busy to take time off."

"I came all this way to see you, and you're not available. What am I supposed to do?"

Go home, Emma thought. She said, "There's a wonderful ranching museum downtown, some great shops, an art gallery, and Daisy Bonner's shop. Enough to keep you busy for hours."

"And tomorrow?"

"I'll look at the schedule and talk to Nacho. Maybe I can take a couple hours between lunch and dinner tomorrow. I'm sure you want to spend time with Koa."

"Of course I want to spend time with my grandson."

"He's on a cattle drive today, Mother. Tomorrow would be much better for both me and Koa. There's a wonderful bakery and coffee shop on the main street. The owner is Linda. The pastries are incredible. You could take a book and spend an hour there."

"I do enjoy excellent coffee and a good Danish."

"It's the only coffee shop on the main street. I'd better get back to work. I'll speak with Nacho about taking a couple hours off tomorrow. Let's talk later this evening, Mother."

"Fine." Pauline ended the call in a resigned voice.

Trace surveyed the tired group of riders who'd spent hours on the cattle drive. They slid to the ground, some testing their wobbly legs, others bending to stretch their backs. Each sported some form of a smile, signaling all had a good experience.

"Trace?"

He glanced behind him to see Barrel approach. "What do you need?"

"Not me. Wyatt and Virgil want to see you in the office. I'll take over out here."

Lifting his hat to shred fingers through his hair, Trace walked to the main lodge.

"Dad. Where are you going?"

"To speak with Wyatt and Virgil. Take care of your horse, then help Barrel."

"Okay."

Trace watched Koa run off, chuckling at the endless energy of youth. Kicking the dirt from his boots, he entered the lodge, walking the short distance to Wyatt's office. He knocked once.

"Come in, Trace."

Shaking their outstretched hands, he took a seat in one of the large leather chairs.

Wyatt leaned forward, resting his arms on the large walnut desk. "How'd the drive go?"

"Good. No accidents, and our guests enjoyed the experience. I'd suggest sending more snacks or packing more for lunch if a cattle drive is on the schedule for next week. The younger guests can put away a lot of food."

Wyatt nodded. "Good idea. Any other ideas?"

"Not really. The group today was athletic and ready for the physical challenges of a drive. Last week, the guests were the opposite, requiring a modified trip. Being flexible would work best."

Virgil shifted on the leather sofa. "A man came by to talk to you this morning, Trace."

"He leave a name?"

Virgil read from a business card. "Charleston Peak. Introduced himself as Chuck."

Groaning, Trace scratched his stubbled jaw. "Chuck is relentless." Reaching out, he took the card from Virgil's outstretched hand. Glancing at it, he shook his head. "He's trying to get me to return to the rodeo. It's not going to happen."

"He asked an odd question, though," Wyatt said. "He inquired about your ranch. I don't recall you telling us about a ranch."

"Family ranch, like here. My dad and mom run it with the help of their foreman. They couldn't do it without him." He didn't mention how he'd added hundreds of acres, a rodeo stock breeding program, and hired one of the best horseman out there as the foreman. Or that his father had already deeded the entire place to Trace, who had the funds for the ever increasing taxes.

"You already know my dad's health is spotty. I may have to take over sooner than I'd first thought. Chuck doesn't want to hear any of it. He's convinced I should return to the rodeo." Shaking his head on a laugh, he stood. "The man's delusional."

"He's coming back later this week to see you," Virgil said.

"It'll be a waste of time. If there's nothing else..." Trace let the unspoken question hang in the air.

"Nope." Wyatt stood. "When will your friend, Sam, be here?"

"Supposed to be here in the morning. I'll confirm. I heard back from another friend. He'd like to come down this weekend to speak with you."

Virgil opened the door. "As good as Sam?"

Trace smiled. "Better."

Chapter Fourteen

Emma had done an excellent job of staying away from Blossom McGuire and her husband, Brent. Five days were left before the guests returned home. Five days for Emma to decide if she had the courage to confront Blossom.

Tonight's activities after dinner would be short, allowing the guests to retreat to their cabins early. It might be the best time to get Blossom alone.

"Don't forget we're offering s'mores at the campfire tonight." Nacho glanced up from his spot at the work counter. "We won't be setting out as many desserts at the dinner buffet."

"Sounds good. I need to ask a favor."

"What is it?" He lifted his cup of coffee, taking a tentative sip.

"My mother's in town. She called yesterday and said she was already on the road. Anyway, I need a couple hours between lunch and dinner tomorrow to visit with her."

"She could come for lunch or stay for dinner. Or have both meals with you tomorrow."

"Dinner in the kitchen with me and Koa would be fine, Nacho."

"Where is she staying?"

"At Helen's in town. I had no idea my mother decided to visit until her phone call yesterday."

"It's not a problem, Emma. Take whatever time you need. We'll make certain everything for both meals is ready well in advance."

"Thanks, Nacho. What else needs to be done for dinner tonight?"

"The ribs are smoked and ready to go into the oven. Beans too. You'll need to prepare a macaroni salad, potato salad, and Caesar salad. Two vegetable trays are already in the refrigerator, as are the desserts. Should be an easy dinner."

Emma slipped into a clean apron, tying it around her waist. "Why don't you go ahead and rest, Nacho. I'll set out the afternoon refreshments and start the setup for dinner."

"I'm going to do that. Thanks."

She knew within ten minutes he'd be asleep, allowing her the private thoughts she'd been ignoring all day. Life had seemed simple a few weeks ago, before complications changed her thinking.

Was it a coincidence Trace, her mother, and Blossom would all be at the ranch at the same time? Was God trying to make a point? Since she didn't believed in coincidences, she leaned toward the latter.

Emma needed to speak with Trace before her mother arrived. They had to be kept away from each other. It felt as if she were caught in some weird version of the Bermuda Triangle.

She turned at the sound of the back door opening. Her breath caught when her gaze landed on the much too handsome cowboy who stood in the doorway.

"Hello, Em."

"Trace. Is there something I can get you?"

"Some of your time, if you have a little to spare." He stepped closer, his caramel colored eyes gentle yet hopeful. Her heart squeezed at the sight of him.

"I have to put out the afternoon refreshments. It may not allow us much time."

"I'll help. Just tell me what to do." He stepped even closer, causing warmth, so long forgotten, to rush through her.

"All right. See the trays over on the counter?" She nodded to her right. "All of those go on the buffet table. I'll bring out the drinks."

They'd tackled the job within ten minutes, closing the door to the dining room behind them. Unless an issue arose, she wouldn't need to return until after the guests had finished.

"Where is a good place to talk?"

She glanced around, already knowing the answer. "I have to stay close, so here is the best." Pulling up a stool, she motioned to a second one. "Do you want something to drink?"

"I'm fine, thanks." The slight tremor in his voice emphasized the same apprehension rolling through her.

Keeping some distance between them, she clasped her hands in her lap and waited. Trace waited until she lifted her head so their gazes could meet.

"Do you remember when we met?"

An odd question, she thought. Emma tried not to dwell on the past and what might've been. Maybe there was a point to Trace's question. Releasing a sigh, she offered a slow nod.

"Yes. I was practicing barrel racing. You stood on the lowest rail of the fence and watched."

"You were the prettiest thing I'd ever seen. You still are, Em."

A lump grew in her throat, making it impossible to answer with words.

"I don't know how you got it into your head that I cheated on you, but I never did. Not once. Ever. Back then, you refused to listen to me. I'm hoping, after all these years, we can talk about your decision to end our marriage."

Squirming on the stool, she considered his wording. *Your decision*, not our decision. He was right. It had been her driving the divorce. Looking back, she realized how childish the decision had been.

The same as now, Emma had no proof, just the word of a woman she didn't know well. She'd allowed pain and anger to control her, not giving Trace a chance to defend himself. Years later, she realized her dreadful mistake.

Unable to meet his questioning caramel eyes, she nodded. "All right."

His shoulders relaxed. "Why did you think I'd been unfaithful?"

"A phone call from a friend. She said you'd been spotted with someone else." Saying it out loud sounded lame. The next would be worse. "Koa and I were staying at my mother's house."

Trace couldn't suppress a groan. "I'm sure she jumped right on it, and encouraged you to file."

"Yes."

"It never happened, Em." Clearing his throat, he stared down at hands scarred from working a ranch and rodeoing. They weren't pretty, but they were clean, as was his conscience.

"I'll admit I wasn't the best husband or father. I practiced hard, spending too many hours getting ready for each rodeo. I told myself we needed money, and the best way to get it was to always walk away with winnings."

"Which you did."

"At the expense of my family. I'd go out with the guys too often, sometimes crashing at a friend's rather than drive home. Mistakes I realized too late." Jaw clenching, he lowered his voice. "If your friend saw me leaving a woman's place, it was because she was past her limit. Me, Jake, or another friend would make sure she got home. I never stayed, Em."

A minute passed, then another without a response.

He leaned closer without touching her. "Emma?"

Swiping at a tear rolling down her cheek, she looked up at him. "I don't know what you want?"

"The truth. Who told you I'd been with someone else?"

Shaking her head, she swiped at another tear. "I don't know why she's important."

"Can you get in touch with her?"

She thought of the residents in cabin six. "Yes."

"After all this time, maybe she'll tell you the truth."

"Doubtful."

"Why?"

"She's never liked me, Trace. Probably why she took so much pleasure in telling me about what happened."

"The point is, nothing happened. She lied, and I want to know why."

Emma understood. She wanted the truth, also. "All right. I'll try. That's the best I can do."

"Would you be more comfortable if I spoke with her? I know how you hate confrontation."

Emma considered his offer. She'd always shied away from uncomfortable conversations, preferring to ignore problems than confront someone. It was how she used to be.

"Thank you, but I have to be the one to talk to her."

"But you'll do it, right?"

"Yes, I'll do it. I know this is important. Koa needs a relationship with you, and I don't want to go through life as your enemy."

"You could never be my enemy, Em." Reaching out, he took her hand in his. "Right now, all I want is the truth."

Walking back to the bunkhouse, he replayed their conversation. It had gone better than he expected. She'd agreed to speak to the woman who played a huge part in ending their marriage.

He wouldn't minimize his part in losing Emma's trust, but he also couldn't ignore her choosing to end their marriage rather than talk about what she'd been told. In truth, she'd shut him out, not answering his calls. Her mother wouldn't allow him in the house to see Emma or Koa. It had been an agonizing time for him.

Once Emma had spoken to the woman who'd lied about his activities, Trace would begin his campaign to win her back.

It wouldn't be an easy task. She had built a life without him, moved out of her mother's home to work at the ranch. Emma had always been a great cook. She could prepare anything, including incredible desserts. He suspected she did the bulk of the cooking for the ranch hands and dude ranch guests, including most of Nacho's secret dishes.

"Hey, Trace." Wyatt jogged up to him. "There's a short ride tomorrow morning to a nearby lake where the guests can fish."

"Right. We'll bring lunches for everyone. What's the tally?"

"All the men and boys are going, and most of the women. The few who prefer to stay here insist they don't need any planned activity. It'll give them time to relax and catch up on their reading. The problem is the following day."

Trace hooked his thumbs in his jeans. "What's the issue?"

"There's a storm coming through. It's moving across Utah now, and is dumping record amounts of rain. I spoke with Virgil, and we want to change things up."

"All right."

"In the morning, Gage is going to lead a tracking exercise. The group will go out in large SUVs and stay somewhat close to the lodge so they can find cover if the storm hits. He offered the class before you arrived and it was well received. What we don't have is anything firm for the afternoon. Any suggestions?"

Trace didn't need to think long. "Have you ever presented a barrel racing demonstration?"

"We've talked about it, but have never been able to pull it together. Do you have anyone in mind?"

"Emma."

"Emma, your...I mean, our cook?"

"She competed in high school and for a while in college."

"Huh, I didn't know that. How long since she competed?"

"Nine years."

"That's a lot of time, Trace."

"Not for a demonstration. Emma won't ride at a competitive speed, but it'll be fast enough for the guests to enjoy it. If the weather holds, she can work with those interested to go through the pattern. She'll need a horse with some experience and three barrels."

"Mandy, a twelve-year-old Paint mare, was trained for barrel racing. We bought her about a year ago. She's our best option." Wyatt waved Virgil over, taking a few minutes to explain Trace's idea.

"She'll need to practice while the guests are with Gage tomorrow morning," Trace said. "I'll talk to Emma and handle setup. What do you guys think?"

Wyatt clasped him on the back. "I think we've got ourselves a new activity."

Chapter Fifteen

"What were you thinking, Trace? I can't possibly be ready to demonstrate barrel racing by tomorrow afternoon." Wiping her hands down what had been a white apron an hour ago, she glared at him. "Nacho and I always begin lunch and dinner preparations right after breakfast. I can't just disappear for a few hours."

"You can disappear as long as you must." Nacho rounded the corner from the pantry. "I ran this kitchen before you arrived, and can certainly take care of things now."

"But—"

He held up his open hand to quiet her. "And don't argue with me, Chica. Wyatt has approved the new activity. You'll do what Trace says."

Stifling a chuckle, Trace saw her jaw drop open, eyes bug out. "That's excellent advice, Nacho. Emma should do whatever I say. That is, whatever is required for a successful barrel racing demonstration. Would you like to see Mandy, the mare you'll be riding?"

When she didn't answer, Nacho spoke again. "Go on. I can finish in here."

Unable to move for several seconds, she looked between the two men before removing her apron and tossing it on the work counter. "Fine. Let's go."

Dinner had ended, yet there was still enough natural light for their trip to the stables. They could hear Barrel and a few others playing guitars, singing around the campfire. Compared to some, it was a quiet night.

Emma kept her distance from Trace as they approached the stables. Spending hours close to him tomorrow morning didn't work with what she already had planned.

Her mother would be driving out from town, expecting to spend much of the day with her and Koa. There'd be little chance Pauline wouldn't spot Trace, and when she did, hiding from her wrath would be impossible.

She should warn Trace tonight so he'd be prepared. The animosity her mother held for Emma's former husband made no sense. She couldn't think of a single person, other than her mother, who disliked him. He made friends easily. Even his most determined competitors enjoyed Trace's company.

The last stall held Mandy, a beautiful Paint mare. "How old is she, Trace?"

"Twelve. Wyatt said they bought her about a year ago. Have you ridden her?"

Emma held out her hand, letting the mare sniff her. "No. I usually ride one of the geldings. Not that I have much time between working and Koa's school activities. Thank you for letting him tag along the last couple weeks."

"No need to thank me. Spending time with Koa is a blessing. He's a great kid. You've done a good job, Emma." There was a wistfulness in his voice she hadn't heard before.

"He's enjoying you being here, Trace. Virgil and Wyatt and the other ranch hands have been great. Having his father here is, well...it's better."

Neither said more for a minute as they absorbed the comments. When Trace spoke, his voice and demeanor were somber.

"I want to start over with you, Em."

"Start over?"

"We lost a lot of time together between me being gone so much and the divorce. I love you and want our marriage back. Unless you're determined to leave our lives as they are."

Emma didn't know how to respond. She wasn't certain letting him know how much she still loved him was the best idea. Keeping the truth from him seemed wrong after he'd been open with her.

"Maybe we could try again, Trace."

"But you're still not certain you can trust me." The resignation in his voice tore at her heart.

"I suppose you're right. Doesn't mean that can't change."

"After you speak to the woman?"

Pressing her lips together, she nodded.

Giving a slow nod, he turned toward Mandy. "What do you think of her, Em?"

"If she's trained for barrel racing, I'm certain she'll be fine. Are you sure the guests would be interested in watching?"

"No doubt. They'll also line up to have you walk them through the pattern. Even the men might be interested, so be prepared." He sent her a smile so sincere it lodged next to her heart. "What do you say?"

Taking a minute, she looked between Mandy and Trace before making her decision. "I'll do it. I just hope you don't regret it."

"Never!" Picking her up, he swung her around before setting her down.

Not letting her go, he stared into her eyes. For an instant, Emma thought he might kiss her. When he pressed a kiss to her forehead and stepped back, a wave of disappointment spread through her.

"You're going to do great."

"I sure hope you're right, cowboy."

Emma rose well before sunrise, nerves pulsing through her. Dressing in jeans and a comfortable long-sleeved shirt, she checked on Koa, still fast asleep, before heading to the kitchen. Starting early would mean getting much of her work finished so Nacho didn't have to do his job as well as hers.

Slipping on her apron, she whipped the egg mixture, prepped the country potatoes, and prepared the pancake batter. Pulling two bowls of muffin mix from the refrigerator, she added fresh blueberries to one and chocolate chips to the other.

Plugging in the juicer, she filled five pitchers with fresh orange juice, and another five with water. Counting scoops of coffee, she prepped for regular and decaf, along with a pot for hot water.

"Thought I heard someone banging around out here." Nacho padded toward her in jeans, a clean shirt, and rubber soled shoes. His hair was combed, though still damp from a shower.

"The noise was worth it, as I've prepped for much of the breakfast. I haven't set out bread for toast or baked the muffins. Koa would love to help you."

"The boy can be my helper anytime, Emma. You've done enough. Go on and meet Trace." He watched her hesitate, then leaned a hip against the counter. "I've been told barrel racing is a lot like riding a bike. Once you've perfected the skill, you can return to it years later."

"I just don't want to embarrass Wyatt or Virgil."

"Or Trace."

Her face turned a slight pink. "Or Trace."

"You won't know until you try. I'll tell you this, those guests will be fine with whatever you show them. Get on now. I have work to do."

Making a stop at her apartment to hustle Koa out of bed, letting him know Nacho would appreciate his help, she grabbed a hat and dug riding gloves from a drawer. Checking herself in the mirror over her dresser, she swallowed the nerves threatening to overcome her.

"You look good, Mom." Koa stifled a yawn while rubbing his eyes. "Where are you going?"

"To the barn. Trace wants me to give the guests a barrel riding demonstration."

He came awake quickly. "Really? I want to watch."

"First, Nacho needs your help with breakfast."

His shoulders dropped, the smile fading. "Ah, Mom..."

"Sorry, kiddo, but he doesn't have anyone else to get food on the buffet table and help the guests. Finish dressing and get to the kitchen. Much of the work is already done, so it won't be hard."

Screwing up his face, Koa scoffed. "None of the work in the kitchen is hard." Stalking back into his bedroom, Emma hid a grin.

"I'm leaving. Don't let Nacho down, son."

"I won't."

The hint of a smile crossed her face as she stepped outside. Crisp morning air stopped her for a moment as she filled her lungs. The sun warmed the chill as she strode to the barn, where lights already brightened the large interior.

Trace stood with Mandy at the far end, his smile at seeing her sent a punch to her gut. She wanted to turn back time, have a redo of the awful day she asked for a divorce. Maybe they could find a way to salvage a relationship she'd helped destroy.

"Morning, Em. Mandy's ready. I've set up the barrels in the far corral."

"So we don't attract too much attention?"

His smile widened. "Exactly. You look ready to ride. Where's Koa?"

"Helping Nacho." Her gaze moved over the mare. "How long since she competed?"

"I don't know. At least a year. She should be perfect for exhibitions. We'll have to decide if putting guests on her back is a good idea."

Emma nodded her understanding while walking around Mandy. "I've seen Margie ride her a few times. Wish I'd paid more attention."

"Best way to check her ability is to get on her back, Em. You ready?"

"Yeah." Her eyes indicated a trepidation her voice concealed.

Walking out the back, they continued to the corral. A couple ranch hands walked past, gave them a second glance, then moved on.

"The distances between barrels is shorter than regulation patterns. You'll start and finish at the open gate, and I won't be timing you." He handed her Mandy's reins.

Emma's mouth opened and closed as she inspected the gear more closely. "This looks just like my saddle. And the reins..." She shot a look at Trace.

"They are yours. I never sold them." His hand moved over the seat to the cantle at the back. "Never could bring myself to let it go."

Throat tight, she stared at him while fighting the burning sensation behind her eyes. "Thank you." She choked the words out, her chest squeezing. Clearing her throat, she walked to the open gate.

Mounting, Emma rode Mandy in a big circle outside the corral before beginning the pattern. She walked the mare around barrel one, then number two, and three before riding to the gate. Repeating the pattern once more at a walk, she increased the speed the third time, and again on the fourth.

"What do you think, Em?"

"She definitely knows what she's doing. It's hard to keep her speed down."

"Increase it when you're comfortable."

Worrying her lower lip, she looked at the barrels. "How far off are we from regulation?"

"At least ten feet for each barrel. We'd need to move you to another location to increase the distance. That's not going to happen today."

"Just gauging how fast I can push her." Leaning forward, she stroked Mandy's neck, her mouth tilting into a grin. "She's a sweet ride."

Trace had seen the look on her face before. Emma was getting back into the game, feeling the excitement of competing.

"Mandy's perfect for you, Em." *So am I*, he thought, keeping the sentiment to himself.

If all went as he hoped, this would be the first step in breaking down her defenses. The first step in winning Emma back.

Chapter Sixteen

"For those of you unfamiliar with this professional rodeo event, the rider will enter the arena, rounding the barrel to her right first. She'll then continue to barrel two, then barrel three. Once around the last one, she'll finish by taking a straight path back through the gate."

Trace shot a look at Emma, whose tense expression atop Mandy signaled her apprehension.

"You all know our rider today. Emma Griffin is one of our cooks, and a veteran of barrel racing since high school. Let's welcome Emma, who's riding Mandy." Trace and the ranch hands around the corral whooped along with the guests.

Encouraging, Trace gave a small nod. Mandy broke into an easy lope, taking a right around the first barrel, and proceeding left around the second and third before speeding back through the open gate. Guests and cowboys cheered, yelled, and clapped. Letting the commotion die down, he gestured with a hand toward Emma.

"That was a perfect example of a barrel race. This event has been part of professional rodeos for a long time, and is included in the National Finals Rodeo each December. They're also included in most smaller, local rodeos.

"Do you want to see her once more?" Affirmative nods and more clapping followed Trace's question. "Emma, are you and Mandy ready?"

Giving him a thumbs up, she waited for his answering nod. Emma took the pattern a little faster this time, yet still not close to what was expected in a competitive event. It didn't matter. The guests shouted their appreciation. She suspected most of them had attended at least one rodeo and knew what to expect. Still, the gratitude of the small crowd brought lightness to her heart.

"Emma is going to stick around for a bit, so anyone who wants to ride the pattern on Mandy should stand over by Emma."

To Trace's surprise, twelve guests, men, women and a few youngsters, formed a line. A hand clasped his shoulder.

"That went real well," Wyatt said. "We should discuss having Emma do it each week."

"Judging by her smile, I'd say she might be open to that." Trace watched the line lengthen, knowing this would be a huge boost to Emma's self-confidence.

"Do you want to talk to her about it?"

"Sure, Wyatt, but as the boss, it might be better coming from you."

"If you think it matters to her, I'll talk to Emma after she finishes here. You'll need to carve out time to work with her during the demonstrations."

"I'm glad to work with her if she agrees. Maybe next year we can prepare an event area so we can use regulation patterns. Just a thought."

"It's worth talking about. Might even add barrel racing to the ranch rodeo and invite a couple local women to enter."

"I'd better go help her out, Wyatt. I'll leave talking to her about making this a regular event to you."

Jogging toward her, Trace's attention moved to a small, gray sedan driving through the ranch entrance. He couldn't see the single occupant. The driver parked in front of a large sign indicating the open area was reserved for trailers loading and unloading horses.

Shaking his head, his steps froze when the driver stepped out of the car. Averting his face as she searched the crowd, he hurried toward Emma.

"Your mother's here." He nodded toward Pauline, who struggled in two-inch heels.

"Oh, no. You need to get out of sight, Trace. If she sees you, well...it won't be pretty."

"I can't hide from her all day, Em."

"She's staying a few hours, will have dinner with Koa and me, then drive back to town. Can't you keep out of sight until she leaves?"

Crossing his arms, he stared down at her. "Why are you so afraid of her?"

Jaw dropping, she quickly recovered, flashing him a withering look. "I am *not* afraid of her. I just don't want her causing a scene in front of the guests. You know better than anyone what she's like when she's riled up. It isn't pretty. I need this job. Just do this today. Please, Trace."

"What if she comes out again? I'm not going to hide every time she shows up. The same as you, I have work to do."

Touching his arm, she pulled it back when realizing what she'd done. "Just today. I'll keep her near the lodge, maybe have her watch Nacho and me work."

"What about Koa? Do you expect him to stay silent about me being at the ranch?"

Catching her lower lip between her teeth, she saw the instant her mother spotted her. "Can you talk to him? She's coming this way, and I still have a few people who want to ride the pattern. Please, Trace. Just this one time, then I'll figure something out."

Blowing out a breath, he dropped his arms, turning a little bit more away from Pauline. "This one time, Em. You'll need to deal with me working here if she comes out again."

"All right. Now hurry, before she spots you." She moved her hands in a swooshing motion. Seeing his lips twitch, she stomped a foot on the hard ground. "Go."

Touching the brim of his hat with a finger, he turned away, determined to find his son. He wasn't sure what he'd say to Koa that wouldn't portray his grandmother in a negative way. Still young and impressionable, he had a lot of time to make up his own mind about Pauline.

Being careful Emma's mother didn't spot him, he headed to the kitchen. Nacho would be heavy into dinner preparations by now. Stepping inside, he nodded at the head cook.

"Hey, Nacho. Any idea where I can find Koa?"

"He ran out of here as soon as breakfast was served. Thought he was going to look for you."

"I didn't see him, but my attention was on Emma."

Nacho looked up from where he cut potatoes for dinner. "How'd she do?"

"Great. Wyatt's going to talk to her about adding the demo to the schedule. Guess I'd better start looking for Koa. If he comes back here, let him know I'm looking for him."

"Will do."

Opening the back door, Trace stepped back a few paces, shutting the door. Glancing behind him, he saw Nacho watching him.

"Emma and Pauline are coming this way."

"You don't want her mother to see you?"

"It'd be best for Emma if she doesn't."

Chuckling, Nacho nodded toward the hallway behind the kitchen. "You'd better go out the back."

"Thanks." He'd just made it to the door when he heard Pauline's voice. Slipping outside, he headed to the barn without looking back.

"Who was that young man you were talking to when I arrived, Emma?"

"What man, Mother?"

"Tall, with broad shoulders. Something about him seemed familiar."

"Must've been one of the ranch hands." Drawing open the door to the kitchen, she motioned her mother to go inside before her. "Nacho, this is my mother, Pauline. Mother, this is Nacho, the ranch's senior chef."

Nacho threw back his head and laughed. "I'm the ranch's cook, ma'am. Don't know anything about being a chef."

"My daughter has talked about your fabulous food. Perhaps you'll consider sharing your recipes with me."

Emma winced. "Mother, I already told you his recipes are family secrets. Sorry, Nacho."

"It's all right, Chica. I do have a very good quesadilla recipe I'd be able to share, ma'am. I'll write it down for you."

Winking at Emma, he opened a drawer, removing paper and a pen. It was their shared joke. Whenever anyone asked, he'd provide a simple quesadilla recipe not even a marginal cook could ruin.

"Here you go." Nacho handed her the recipe.

A wide smile spread across her face as she clutched the recipe to her chest. "Thank you, Nacho."

"Come on, Mother. I'll give you a tour."

"Who I'd like to see is my grandson. Where is Koa?"

Emma waved a hand in the air. "You know how he is. If we don't run across him first, he'll definitely be in the kitchen for dinner."

"Aren't we eating in the dining room?"

"Unfortunately, no, Mother. The guests eat in there. We'll have dinner here at the cozy table in the corner. It's actually very nice." Risking a glance outside, she released a stress-filled breath.

Trace spoke with Koa at the far end of the large barn. Both looked so serious she had to suppress a grin. If her mother hadn't called her name, Emma could've watched them the rest of the day. Father and son, two males who'd bonded, and would do anything for the other.

"Emma, what are you looking at?"

Whirling around, she took her mother's arm, guiding her to the hallway behind the kitchen. "I haven't shown you our apartment."

Pauline's nose wrinkled. "You live here, like a servant?"

"No, Mother. Like an employee who gets an apartment as part of my job." She shoved the door open. "Go on in. It's not big, but it suits Koa and me."

Walking through the compact living room, Pauline continued down the hall. It was easy to pick out Emma's bedroom with its cream colored bedspread and half a dozen throw pillows. Books filled shelves on one side of the double bed, while a small desk filled the space on the other side.

The closest didn't hold a lot. A few pairs of jeans, black slacks, blouses, and three cotton dresses. Boots, tennis shoes, sandals, and thick-soled work shoes took up the floor space. Not much, yet she'd always gotten by with little.

Emma moved out of her way when Pauline walked to the second bedroom. Koa's room was smaller with a twin bed, dresser, and desk. His clothes were folded and piled on top of a trunk at the foot of the bed. The spread and curtains were made of his favorite color, red. He'd picked it out at two years old and never wavered.

The bath was a decent size, with a shower and tub combo. Clean and neat, Pauline recognized the towels as a set a neighbor had given Emma when she married Trace. Her stomach twisted at the thought of her ex-son-in-law.

Emma and Koa were much better off without him.

Chapter Seventeen

"I understand, Dad. Grandma doesn't know you're here. If she did know, she'd be mad at Mom." Koa shot a look at the back of the lodge. "Grandma gets mad about a lot of stuff."

He stared at the ground a moment before lifting his head. "I know Grandma doesn't like you."

Trace wasn't sure how to respond. He hadn't expected Koa to be familiar with Pauline's feelings about him.

"Grandma can be real grumpy about stuff. She doesn't like cowboys or the rodeo or anyone who works for rodeos. I don't know why she came here today. She hates horses and cows."

Pushing his hat back on his forehead, Trace took Koa's shoulders. "Grandma is here because she misses you and your mom. She loves you enough to come to a place she doesn't like to spend time with you. My guess is she's probably wondering where you are."

Giving a grudging nod, Koa didn't move. "Who will you sit with at dinner if I'm with Mom and Grandma?"

His throat tightened at his son's concern. "Don't worry about me. I'll sit with the other ranch hands." Trace knew Emma hadn't planned for Pauline to spend the night. "You may eat a little early so Grandma doesn't have to drive back to town in the dark."

Koa's eyes brightened. "Then we can sit around the campfire and make s'mores."

"If it's all right with your mom."

"Mom can make one too. She loves chocolate."

Trace remembered that about her. Chocolate anything—ice cream, cream pie, caramel and nut squares, cookies, cake, candy, and s'mores. He liked the idea of her sitting with them, roasting marshmallows before slipping one onto a graham cracker holding a square of chocolate.

"You can invite her, Koa."

"She never comes."

"What does she do while everyone is gathered around the fire?"

Koa looked at him, a mischievous grin forming. "Soaks her feet."

Laughing, Trace turned his son toward the lodge. "Go on and see your grandma. I'll be at the campfire later."

Taking off, Koa turned and waved. "See ya, Dad."

Trace couldn't move. He didn't want to do anything except watch his son step safely inside the lodge. Once the door closed, he turned away, sucking in a deep breath. How would he ever walk away from Koa if Emma refused to give him another chance?

Masking deep feelings for the two people he loved, Trace stalked to the bunkhouse. A shower, clean clothes, and dinner were in order. And staying out of Pauline's sight.

He could only imagine the scene she'd create if she spotted him. It would be loud and ugly, jeopardizing his job, and would embarrass Emma. The last was unacceptable.

"Hey, Trace." Wyatt joined him at the long table outside the bunkhouse. "What's the deal with your friend, Sam? He never showed up. And have you heard from the other guy about when he can be here?"

"Geez, I'm sorry, Wyatt. Sam ran into a problem and will be here tomorrow. Jake Kelman will arrive on Saturday. I meant to tell you sooner. Too much going on."

Wyatt lifted a brow. "Like Emma's mother showing up?"

"Pauline doesn't know I'm working here. It won't be pretty if she finds out."

"Met her after dinner in the kitchen. She mentioned driving back to town tonight. But I expect she'll be back before going home. I'd suggest you be vigilant."

"I don't want this to cause you trouble, Wyatt."

"It won't. Tomorrow, you'll be with the group riding out to the river. Some will fish, others will take a short hike. Gage will give a short presentation on the area, the fauna and flora. After lunch, you'll ride back. The group will be gone most of the day. I'll talk to Emma and make sure she keeps her mother in the lodge mid to late afternoon. Maybe I can get her to head into town and show her around."

"What about Nacho? He'll need help."

"Seems one of our guests is a chef. Has a degree from one of the famous schools. She asked about working alongside Nacho, and he said it was fine with him."

"Then that's what I'll talk to Emma about, Wyatt. Have her drive into town after breakfast and spend the day with her mom. Come back after dinner. Assuming it's all right with you."

"Fine. That way we don't have to worry about your friend, Sam, showing up for an interview. I had hoped you'd give him a tour."

"No problem. I'll talk to Emma as soon as Pauline leaves."

Wyatt clasped Trace's shoulder. "Thanks, man. And be sure to take part in the campfire. Wouldn't want you to miss out on the s'mores."

Chuckling, he watched as the guests began to leave the lodge after dinner. They usually took walks or returned to their cabins before wandering to the campfire. Tonight, the children will put on a skit, guests will sing with the ranch hands, and Barrel will do a few of his magic tricks. The evening will end with s'mores and a few other treats from the kitchen. To most, it would seem a pretty sedate night, yet it continued to be one of the guests' favorites.

Staying partway in the shadows, Trace kept an eye on the lodge, hoping to see Emma and Pauline. Koa was already outside, playing with a few of the younger guests.

He had to give it to his boy, not once had he come close to or acknowledged his father.

Movement at the lodge caught his attention. Emma walked out with her mother. They stayed on the flagstone path on the way to Pauline's rental car. They didn't spend much time talking outside the car before she climbed inside and drove off.

Trace joined Emma as the car's taillights disappeared around a bend in the road. Stopping behind her, he placed his hands on her shoulders, feeling her tense, then relax.

"Are you all right?" He dropped his hands when she turned to face him.

"Yes, and no. I've never been able to relax around her. Not as a child, and not as an adult." Her chuckle held no humor. "Being around her wears me out, Trace." Her gaze dropped to the ground.

When her shoulders sagged, he braced them with his hands. "Take a couple deep breaths, the same as you used to do."

Raising her head, tired eyes met his. "Doesn't always work." Instead of breaking the connection, she continued to stare into his warm caramel eyes, wishing she could turn back the clock.

That's why she didn't move away when his head slowly lowered, hovered above her lips for an instant before his mouth covered hers. Tentative at first, he deepened the kiss, his body remembering the feel and taste of her. When her hands ran up his arms and around his neck, he felt as if he'd come home.

Knowing they had to stop, he raised his head, pressed another quick kiss to her mouth, and slowly put a few inches between them.

"I've wanted to do that for a very long time." His voice broke on the emotion rolling through him.

"So have I."

Taking another chance, he wrapped his arms around her. Holding her tight, he rested his chin on the top of her head. Neither spoke, allowing themselves a few minutes alone before stepping away.

Cupping her face in both hands, he brushed a soft kiss across her lips. "I want another chance with you, Emma." Seeing her eyes tear, he tugged her against his chest. "We can go as slow as you want. Just let me make things right with you and Koa."

Blossom McGuire stood outside the cabin she shared with her husband, Brent, watching Emma and Trace. The sorrow on their faces twisted her stomach, creating hot tears to stream down her cheeks.

If she'd said no when asked to lie about Trace, they never would've divorced, may have even had more children. Too bad she couldn't turn back time, refuse to say the words which destroyed their marriage.

Blossom thought back on the day the hundred dollar bill had been waved before her. She'd been broke, with a total of fifty cents in her pocket. The money offered would get her through a couple weeks. She recalled thinking a job would become available by then. The hundred was her lifeline.

Back then, there'd been another reason to accept the money. Blossom had always wanted Trace to notice her. All his attention had been focused on Emma. No other woman could compete with the petite, brown-haired beauty.

His actions after Emma demanded a divorce were unexpected. Instead of hitting the bars and picking up women, as some men would do, he'd withdrawn into himself. Days were spent traveling for rodeo appearances, using the gym, or meeting with sponsors. His friends stayed close, providing a support system Blossom had never experienced.

Instead of satisfaction at the part she'd played in ending his marriage, shame and guilt plagued her. She'd been stunned to find Emma and Trace working at the dude ranch.

As the week passed, Blossom became more convinced she'd been brought to Whistle Rock Ranch to apologize, maybe find a way to make amends. Watching them hold each other, Trace whispering close to Emma's ear, Blossom decided tonight wasn't the time for her mea culpa.

"Hey, sweetheart." Brent joined her on the small porch of the cabin. "Do you want to take a walk, then join everyone at the campfire?"

Gaze locking on her husband, Blossom smiled, thankful for all she'd been given. Brent was a wonderful man. He'd saved his rodeo winnings, putting the money into his ranch in Montana. They were already planning for children, and Blossom was pursuing her interest in medicinal herbs.

"That sounds wonderful." Taking his outstretched hand, she let him steer her toward the corral containing two and three-year-old Paints. "Will we be breeding horses at our ranch?"

"Mainly cattle, but some horses. I'm going to talk to Wyatt about buying three or four horses from his herd. They're the best Paints bred in the country. Have you spoken with Emma yet?"

Sucking in a breath, Blossom shook her head. "Not yet. I'm planning to tell her soon."

There were days she regretted telling Brent about what she considered her deal with the devil. But she'd made the decision to start their life together without deceit. He'd been open about transgressions which shamed him. She could do no less.

"The sooner you admit what happened, the sooner you'll start healing, sweetheart." He squeezed her hand.

"I know," she breathed out.

"I'll be right there with you, Blossom. It's going to be all right."

"Thank you, Brent. Your support means a lot to me." Once again, she stared up at her husband, wondering what she'd done to deserve such an amazing man.

Chapter Eighteen

Sam Miller slid from the seat of the four-wheel drive truck, landing on the ground with a thud. Being five-foot-four made some activities more difficult, taking a little more time and effort. Good thing giving up wasn't in her vocabulary.

"May I help you?" Jimmy French walked toward her, white teeth flashing in a smile.

"I'm Sam Miller. I'm looking for Trace Griffin."

"He's out with the guests. Should be back in," he checked his phone, "an hour. You're welcome to wait in the lodge. I'll have Nacho get you whatever you want to drink. If you're hungry—"

"Nacho?"

"The ranch's cook. I'll introduce you." Jimmy headed toward the lodge.

Hurrying to catch up, Sam looked around, impressed with the number and condition of the buildings. The website gave all the pertinent information, but the pictures didn't show the true beauty of the ranch with an incredible view of the Tetons.

The kitchen was another welcome surprise. Equipped with the latest appliances, there was plenty of room for several workers.

"Good morning, Emma."

"Hey, Jimmy." She walked up to his companion, holding out her hand. "I'm the assistant cook, Emma."

"Sam. I'm here to see Trace about a job."

Emma checked the time. "He'll be back in about an hour or so. Can I get you something to drink or eat?"

"Water would be great. Trace did say I'd be meeting with Wyatt Bonner and Virgil Redstar."

"I'm going to take off." Jimmy touched the brim of his hat. "Good meeting you, Sam."

"Same here. Hope to see you around the ranch."

Handing Sam the water, Emma washed and dried her hands. "Unless you want to wait for Trace, I can hunt down Wyatt and Virgil."

"If you don't mind, I'd prefer to wait for Trace. He's the one who recommended me."

"I don't mind at all. Nacho is working on some kind of fix for our outdoor grill, so for now, we have the kitchen to ourselves. Are you here for a ranch hand position?"

"That, and to work with the dude ranch guests. Trace thought coming on now would give me some time to learn what is offered and my duties before the season ends."

Slicing a loaf of bread, Emma spread each piece with a butter and garlic mixture. "Did you work with him at the rodeo?"

"Yes and no." Uncapping the bottle of water, Sam took a long swallow. "He was a competitor while I worked with the stock contractors. Trace would come around and check the horses, asking real good questions."

Emma lifted a brow. "How so?"

"His questions were always well thought out. He was always real interested in each of the horses. This may sound strange, but some of the riders had no interest in learning about the horse they'd drawn. Of course, some of the men were shy. Those were the ones who listened and asked questions of other riders. Not Trace. He spent a good amount of time checking out the animals."

Wrapping the buttered loaves in foil, Emma set them aside. "He's always been an inquisitive guy." Opening the refrigerator, she removed tomatoes, cucumbers, three different kinds of greens, and cheese.

"Have you known him long?"

Emma wasn't certain how to answer, or how much Sam already knew about them. "Quite a while." Chopping the tomatoes, she glanced out the window, seeing Trace dismount with the others. "The riders have returned. He should be here soon."

Sam swiveled in the chair, seeing Trace through the window. "I'll head out to let him know I'm here."

"Good idea. It could be a while before he comes to the lodge." Emma watched Sam leave the kitchen and approach Trace.

She saw the instant he spotted his friend. A broad smile appeared as he held out his hand. They shook, then he pulled Sam into a quick hug. It was so Trace. He never hesitated to show affection.

Emma thought of their kiss and his plea to try again. She still loved him, wanted to agree. Her hesitancy came from how her mother would respond. Pauline Bullard's anger would be swift and ugly, and she wouldn't care who was around when the eruption occurred.

She had to speak with Blossom, discover if the woman lied or told the truth about Trace. Setting aside the salad fixings, Emma wiped both hands down her apron. Looking through the window, her gaze locked on Blossom and Brent.

Holding hands, the couple looked as if they faced no problems. Emma let out a deep sigh. She couldn't remember a time when her rocky marriage didn't cause stress. At least for her.

Trace hadn't hit the level of winnings he did after the divorce. They weren't poor. The truth was, they were better off than at least eighty percent of the other married competitors. Yet her mother never stopped harping about their lack of money.

"I was a fool to listen to her," Emma mumbled.

She and Trace earned more than enough for a rental home, food, clothes, and a babysitter for the occasional night out. A new sponsor gave him a tricked out truck. Except for all the nights he came home late, all seemed to be going well.

It was her mother who began chipping away at the already troubled relationship. For a long time, Emma refused to listen. She visited her mother less often, leaving Koa with a babysitter when she did stop by. Instead of slowing her criticism of Trace, Pauline became more vocal.

It was during this time that Blossom called, almost giddy to share the news about Trace.

She jumped when the kitchen door flew open, Trace walking to her. "Hey, Emma. I guess you've already met Sam."

"I have."

"Jimmy said Wyatt and Virgil are in the office." He turned to Sam. "It's time for you to meet the bosses." He shot a warm smile at Emma before leading Sam through the lodge to the office.

"What should I know about them?"

Trace stopped to face Sam. "Wyatt is part of the family which started Whistle Rock Ranch. Virgil is his closest friend, and has pretty much taken over the foreman position from his father, Jasper."

"Jasper retired?"

"No. He was diagnosed with adult asthma and instructed to slow down. Similar to Wyatt's father, Anson, who suffered a heart attack a few months ago and had to cut back on his activities. "He had to pass the baton to his son. I've found Wyatt and Virgil to be fair and clear in their vision for the ranch. I didn't have high expectations about working the dude ranch, but it has turned out well."

"What about your ranch?"

Unable to suppress a wince, Trace looked toward the office, then returned his attention to Sam. "They don't know I own it. I'd appreciate it if you'd let me tell them when the time is right."

Sam gave a knowing nod. "Whatever you want. It's your decision."

"Thanks. Might as well get this over with." Knocking, he waited until Wyatt called out.

"Come on in."

Opening the door, Wyatt walked in with Sam on his heels. "Wyatt, Virgil, this is Sam Miller."

Stunned silence gripped the room before both men stood. Wyatt recovered first, walking up to Sam, his hand outstretched. "Hello, Sam. Can I assume your full name is Samantha?"

Pauline sat in her hotel room, brooding about not having complete access to Emma and Koa. She'd seen her grandson a total of thirty minutes since traveling all the way here.

The friends who'd brought her had their own plans, including trips to Jackson, Yellowstone, and other sights Pauline would love to see. Places she'd assumed Emma would show her, but her selfish daughter hadn't offered.

"After all I've done for her, she can't even take a few days off to spend with her mother." Saying the words out loud fueled the anger which had built since notifying Emma she was on her way to Brilliance.

Pauline was tired of eating her meals and spending the rest of each day alone. Ever since the divorce from Emma's stepfather, it had been difficult to break free of what the doctor called low-level depression. He'd prescribed medication, which helped somewhat, but still left her feeling down and anxious.

She hadn't expected the end of her second marriage. Although his job kept him traveling, he seemed happy. Maybe if she'd agreed to have the children he wanted, it would've worked out. Or it could've left her with two or three additional mouths to feed and no father. Regardless, other than Emma and Koa, Pauline was alone.

Shoving up from the bed, she paced to the window. Stars sparkled in the inky black night. She'd love to go for a walk. Lacking a companion, she opted to stay inside. Other than herself, the parlor, with a large selection of games and books, was empty, as was the adjoining room with a large, flatscreen television.

After several minutes in each room, with no one joining her, Pauline took the stairs to her room and began to fret. Too early to go to bed, and too late to drive out to the ranch.

The ranch had her stymied. She knew the kitchen job had become important to Emma, and Koa loved being around horses and riding. He'd been doing well in school, and according to Emma, had quite a few friends.

Yet Pauline couldn't shake the feeling something was going on. While visiting with Koa, her grandson kept looking around, as if expecting someone, or glancing at his mother for some type of guidance. Regardless, his attention certainly wasn't where it should be—on his grandmother.

The answer to her loneliness seemed simple. Rummaging through her purse, she pulled out the phone.

A cursory check of the time told her Emma would still be awake. Tapping her daughter's number, she held the phone to her ear. One, two, three...six rings before she heard the familiar voice message.

Frustrated at not reaching Emma, she hung up and tried again. As before, the call triggered the voice message. This time, Pauline left a message.

"Emma, I'll be coming to the ranch tomorrow after lunch. I expect you and Koa will find time to visit. I'd prefer to stay for dinner before driving back to town. I'll see you tomorrow."

Emma waited until the call ended before listening to the message. She'd expected her mother to visit again, but hoped it would be between breakfast and lunch. Should she call her back? At this point, it would be best for her mother to come when it was convenient.

"You all right?" Trace's arm tightened around her shoulders. They'd been sitting on one of several benches staring as the campfire faded into embers. Koa was with the other children, watching a movie in the lodge. It gave them time to talk without interruption.

"It's Mother. She's driving out tomorrow after lunch." She leaned against him. "What are you doing tomorrow afternoon?"

"Gage is taking a group of guests on a hike up to the falls right after lunch. It's for those more experienced who want to push their limits. I plan to go with them."

"Doesn't sound as if it would be appropriate for Koa."

"Not this one, Em. No one under eighteen is going. I've been up the trail before, and it's not close to expert level, but does require more experience and confidence than the previous hikes." He pressed a kiss to her temple.

"You'll be careful, right?"

A mischievous grin appeared. "You aren't worried about me, are you?"

She gave a quick shake of her head. "Of course not." But her features didn't support the denial. "I've learned you can do anything. Your son calls you a superhero."

Trace chuckled at the comment. "He does not."

"Sure does. He wants to be just like you when he grows up."

Falling into silence, Trace thought of all they'd been through, wishing he'd approached Emma's demand for a divorce differently. If he'd forced more discussion, they might not be going through the painful process of trying to rebuild their relationship.

"You know, eventually your mother will discover we're seeing each other. When that happens, she'll fight us, the same as before."

Emma knew what he wasn't saying. If she'd been stronger, more mature a few years earlier, she and Trace might never have gone through the painful divorce. She wanted to believe it wouldn't have happened now. Which reminded her about speaking to Blossom before she left on Sunday.

"This time will be different, Trace." Emma's stomach clenched at the doubt in his eyes. "I promise you, my mother won't be the one to ruin what could be our second chance."

Chapter Nineteen

"Are you certain Robber won't come back again and try to raise the price?" Trace adjusted the phone against his ear to cut out as much noise as possible while maintaining his privacy.

"That's the thing with Robber," Augie Pride responded. His foreman and Robert Folton had known each other most of their lives, which prompted Trace to make Augie the lead in negotiations for the rodeo stock company. "Until the deal is signed and notarized, nothing's set in stone."

"Has he signed our latest offer?"

"Yep. I drove over to his operation yesterday and picked it up. Not that I don't trust the man." Augie barked out a laugh. "You'll need to call the attorney and bank to get the process going. I'm sending you the signed agreement via text, but will get copies to anyone you want once I get the word."

"Thanks, Augie. This is great news. First item is getting updated financials from Robber or his accountant."

"I already told him we'd need them right away. He's pretty motivated. The new wife wants to take an extended vacation. She basically told him he'd better be ready in six weeks or she'd take off without him."

"Robber always does better with a deadline. When do I need to be there?"

"You'll want to get back up here within a few weeks. Robber's head of operations and the woman in charge of rodeo relations are talking retirement when their boss leaves."

"Aren't they married?" Trace remembered celebrating their anniversary at one of the rodeos a couple years back. He didn't know either, but stopped by to congratulate them.

"Sure are. Rockiest union I've ever seen, but it works for Hal and Bitsy. They're getting up in years, so you may want to bring in your own people."

"I'd want to negotiate for them to stay long enough to train their replacements."

"I'm sure they'll agree to that. Rumor has it they're thinking of moving to Arizona to be close to their grandkids."

"Keep me posted, Augie. Do you still want a piece of the stock company action?" The foreman had mentioned several times his interest in investing some of his savings in the deal.

"I've been thinking on it. We'll talk when you get up here."

"Works for me. I'd better get going. Keep me posted."

"Will do, boss."

Hiding the excitement Augie's call triggered, Trace slid the phone away. If all went well, he'd be the owner of Folton Stock Company within weeks.

The purchase would mean he'd have to quit his job at Whistle Rock Ranch. The biggest problem facing him would be talking Emma into leaving with him. Trace would move out of the big house where his parents lived, allowing Emma and Koa to move in with them until they married. Trace wasn't worried about a place to stay. If needed, he'd stay at the Folton Stock Company offices. What he didn't want was her deciding to stay at Whistle Rock after the season ended.

"Dad!"

The sound of his son's voice had him whirling around. "Morning, Koa."

"Morning. Are you going on the hike with Gage this afternoon, 'cause I want to go?"

"Sorry, buddy. You're going to stay behind on this one."

"But Daaaad," he groaned. "I can hike."

"I know you can, but this one is for guests eighteen and older. None of the kids are going, and that includes the teenagers."

Shoving hands in his pockets, Koa's lower lip jutted out. "Then what am I going to do this afternoon?"

"Barrel and Jimmy are taking those not on the hike to the lake for a swim. The water has warmed up enough you won't freeze your butt off."

Koa burst into laughter. "Mom wouldn't like you saying that."

Ruffling his son's hair, Trace chuckled. "Probably not. What are you doing this morning?"

"Mom says I can help her and Nacho get lunch ready or hang out with you. Can I? Hang out with you I mean?"

"Definitely. After breakfast, I'm doing a demonstration on tacking up horses for trail rides and could use your help."

He shoved a fist into the air. "Great!"

"All right. Let's eat, then we can get ready for the demonstration." Trace walked toward the buffet table outside the bunkhouse. Most of the men were already filling their plates, and the aroma of bacon caused his stomach to growl.

Koa reached up, patting his father's stomach while giggling. Trace couldn't stop a chuckle of his own. Out of the corner of his eye, he spotted a nondescript sedan approaching the entrance to the ranch. Dismissing it as a local coming to check on their boarded horse, he got in the food line, motioning Koa ahead of him.

Plates filled with eggs, pancakes, bacon, sausage, and biscuits with jam, they found seats among the other ranch hands. Koa ate as if it was no big deal being a nine-year-old among men in their twenties and thirties.

In truth, it wasn't an issue. They treated him as an equal, asking questions, laughing at some of his jokes. Eating in silence, listening to the banter, Trace couldn't stop himself from hoping his ranch and stock operation ran as well as the Bonner ranch. It all came down to those he hired, and that would be on him and Augie.

Glancing to the end of the table, he spotted Sam talking to Jimmy French. After the initial surprise, Wyatt and

Virgil interviewed her the same as any applicant. Thirty minutes sped by. The end result being the ranch had a new employee. Reminding himself he needed to call Jake, find out why his closest friend hadn't showed up, Trace went back to eating.

Loud shouts from outside the kitchen had the men turning their attention to three people, their features hard as their voices rose. Trace's shoulders slumped as his anger rose.

Pauline Bullard, fisted hands on hips, stood within inches of Emma, shouting her displeasure. Nacho tried to get between them, but Pauline kept shoving him out of her way. Finally, Nacho planted himself before her, his chin out, arms crossed.

Steel in his voice, he glared at the older woman. "You will not talk to Emma that way."

"She's my daughter."

"Then you should act like a loving mother," Nacho shot back.

"What's going on?"

Pauline turned toward the familiar voice, her features feral. "You!"

Doing his best to remain neutral, Trace moved in front of Emma. "Yeah, Pauline. It's me. How have you been?"

"Trace, I can handle my mother." Emma moved in front of him, glaring at Pauline. "You should leave. We'll talk after you've gone home."

"We'll talk now, Emma. I want to know what he's doing here." She pointed a finger at Trace's chest. No one could miss the sneer in her voice.

"Trace works here."

"Then I'll speak to the owners, let them know what kind of man he is."

"I don't know what you could possibly say to change their minds, Mother. They are thrilled with his work. Now turn around and drive away before you embarrass yourself more than you already have."

Straightening, Pauline looked between Emma and Trace. "Do not tell me you two are considering remarrying."

A slight smile curved Trace's lips before Emma answered. "We're talking. The rest is none of your business."

Throwing her head back to stare at the sky, Pauline let out an almost animalistic groan. Not sure how to react, Trace put a steadying hand on her elbow. Wrenching it from his grasp, she stepped away.

"Don't you ever touch me."

"Dad? What's happening?" Koa's voice brought some calm to the anger erupting from Pauline.

"We're having a difference of opinion, buddy."

Whirling around, Koa looked up at Pauline. "Why do you hate my dad, Grandma?"

When Pauline opened her mouth to answer, Emma stepped closer. "Don't say anything you will later regret, Mother." Leaning forward, she spoke in her ear. "Don't speak a word against Trace or you'll never see me or Koa again."

"You wouldn't," the older woman hissed.

"I would, so don't push me. Either you calm down and talk in a rational manner, or you'll have to go back to town."

"What's happening in here?"

Trace winced at Virgil's voice. The ranch didn't need their guests witnessing a family's meltdown.

"Virgil, this is my mother, Pauline Bullard. She's staying in town a few days and drove out for a visit."

Removing his hat, he held out a hand. "Pleasure meeting you, Mrs. Bullard. I'm Virgil Redstar, foreman of Whistle Rock Ranch."

Glancing between Emma and Trace, Pauline accepted his hand. "Good to meet you, Mr. Redstar."

"Call me Virgil. We sure are glad to have Emma working for us. Can't imagine anyone better suited for the difficult job of feeding guests and ranch hands. Everyone loves her." He looked at Koa. "And they're real fond of this rascal."

"Hey," Koa responded with a smile.

"Will you be joining us for today's activities? There's a hike up to the falls this afternoon. Or we could tack up a horse for you to ride."

Face coloring, Pauline shook her head. "No. No. I wouldn't want to be a bother. Besides, I'm meeting friends for lunch in town. Right, Emma?"

"Whatever you say, Mother." The clipped words were said without rancor.

"Well then, I'll let you get back to your conversation. Hope to see you at the ranch before you leave town, Mrs. Bullard."

"Thank you, Virgil."

Letting out a silent breath, Trace kept his voice low. "Pauline, why don't you stay for a bit and talk to Emma? No sense driving back to town angry."

"I am not angry, and I won't be staying." Shifting, she faced Emma. "I'll be back before leaving town so we can work out what could be a disaster for everyone."

Standing twenty feet away, Blossom listened to the exchange, feeling rotten. If she hadn't called Emma, told her the lie, which she'd been paid to pass along, the scene this morning would've never happened.

Taking a few tentative steps, she felt Brent grip her arm. "Not now. You want to talk to Emma and Trace without her mother present. Plus, they all need to cool down."

"I just want to get it over with."

"I know, Blossom. Now isn't the time."

"We're only here another two days, Brent. I have to do this before we leave."

"Later today, after I get back from the hike. Emma's mother may be gone by then. You don't want to explain with her around."

Nodding, she laid her hand over his. "You're right. I just can't stand that I had a part in what's happening."

"I know, sweetheart. Trust me. We'll do what we can to make it right before leaving for home."

Chapter Twenty

The cough had started small, growing over the hours since dawn. Walking through the barn, Jasper bent at the waist, trying to relieve the congestion enough to breathe.

The inhaler provided no relief, neither had the meds. If Monica or Virgil noticed, they'd rush him to the hospital, which would ruin what had been a great week.

Until this morning, he'd experienced the usual congestion and coughing. Nothing close to what was happening now. The sense his knees were failing had him grasping the top edge of a stall in time to stop himself from dropping to the ground.

He needed to get back to his apartment, take another dose of meds, and try his backup inhaler. If he could stay at his current spot long enough to regain his strength, he might be able to cross the distance without anyone noticing.

"Hey, Pop. You got a minute to help me move some old tack?" Virgil approached from the back of the barn. When Jasper didn't answer, Virgil picked up his pace. "Pop?"

Instead of answering, Jasper began another bout of coughing, his face turning a purple-red as he struggled to breathe.

Wrapping an arm around his father's waist, Virgil began walking toward the apartment, stopping when Jasper's coughing spasms worsened.

"When did this start?"

Jasper clasped his son's arm, choking out a response. "Inhaler...isn't....working."

"You took your meds?"

"Yes. Need water."

"We're almost to my truck. There are bottles of water in the back seat." Virgil could feel his father's body tense under his hold. "I'm taking you to the hospital."

"No."

"You don't have a choice."

Jasper's attempt to dig in his heels failed as another coughing fit racked his body. Reaching the truck, Virgil helped his father inside before running around to the driver's side and leaving for the hospital.

"Do you have the inhaler with you?"

Dragging it from a pocket, Jasper held it up before another coughing fit took over and the inhaler dropped to the floor.

Heart pounding, Virgil's hands grew damp as he cut the distance to the hospital. Pulling into the lot, he came to a screeching halt in front of the entrance.

Waving to the lone security guard, the two helped Jasper out of the truck. Reaching the double glass doors, an orderly came toward them, pushing a wheelchair.

"I will walk."

"You're riding in the chair, Pop, and no complaining." Entering the emergency room, Virgil spotted James Ryan, the same doctor who'd treated Jasper when the first episodes of adult asthma occurred months earlier.

"What's going on, Mr. Redstar?" Doctor Ryan addressed Jasper, though he wasn't surprised when Virgil answered.

"He can't breathe. Neither the inhaler nor meds seem to be working."

"All right. Let's get him in an examination cubicle. Virgil, do you mind waiting in the hall? We'll come and get you as soon as I know something."

"Pop, don't you give the doctor any problems. Okay?"

Jasper coughed, glaring at Vigil as he waved a hand in the air. Shaking his head, Virgil chuckled as he walked into the hall. Sliding his phone from his pocket, he hit speed dial for his wife.

"Hey, Virg. What's up?" He could hear the smile in Lily's voice.

"Pop had another episode. We're in the emergency room."

"I'm on my way."

"Lily?" But he was too late. Seconds later, Lily approached him in the hall.

Pressing a kiss to Virgil's lips, she glanced toward the emergency door. "Who's with him?"

"Dr. Ryan."

"Good. He's already familiar with Jasper's history. What happened?"

Explaining what he knew, Virgil shoved hands in his pockets. "My guess is he's been struggling all day. The old fool could've died if I hadn't found him in the barn."

Placing a hand on his shoulder, Lily squeezed. "He's as stubborn as you, sweetheart."

Snorting, he stared at the floor. "You're right. I'm sure our children will be just as stubborn."

Lily grinned, taking his hand in hers. "Just my luck."

They wanted two or three children at some point. For now, they were still getting to know each other after years apart.

A nurse Virgil hadn't seen before walked toward them. "Mr. Redstar? Oh, hi, Lily. This must be your husband."

Lily nodded. "Virgil, this is Cindy Walmer, our newest nurse. She's been assigned to the Emergency Department."

"Nice to meet you, Cindy. How's my father?"

"You can come back now. Doctor Ryan wants to speak with you."

Taking Virgil's hand, Lily walked beside him to where Jasper sat on the edge of the bed. He glanced up to acknowledge their presence, his features impassive.

"How is he, doc?" Virgil looked him over, noticed he wasn't coughing.

"He's fine for now. We had a serious talk about his work, and what he'll need to do to control the asthma attacks. I'm afraid it wasn't what your father wanted to hear. Am I right, Mr. Redstar?"

"You know darn well it wasn't." Jasper shot a look at Virgil. "He wants me to quit my job and take a long vacation. Crazy. I can't just walk away."

"Maybe it's time for you and Mom to take off for a while. We have relatives near Salt Lake City and Seattle. You could visit them for a while. What do you think, doc?"

"Those two are good choices. There are others you might want to consider. I'll write out a list. I'm changing inhalers and upping the dosage of his other meds. What's most important is rest and to get away from the ranch. The dust and dirt don't help him."

"Not that I'm not thankful for what you've done, Doc Ryan, but can I get out of here?" Jasper slid off the bed, using a hand to steady himself when his feet touched the floor.

"Pick these up at the pharmacy before leaving for the ranch." James handed him prescriptions. "I want to see you again in a week."

"I don't have time—"

Virgil interrupted his father. "He'll be here."

"At my office. Call to get a specific time."

"Will do. Thanks, Doc Ryan."

The doctor shifted to spear Jasper with a penetrating look. "Get to the hospital if you experience any further attacks. You've had it long enough to know when something isn't right."

"Fine," Jasper mumbled.

"I'll keep better track on what's going on with him. So will Monica."

Jasper glared at Virgil. "I don't want her to know."

"You can't keep this from her, Pop." Not wanting to argue in front of Doc Ryan, he put a steadying hand on his father's arm. "Let's get you home."

"I can't believe you took him to the hospital without me." Monica sat on a chair next to Jasper's bed, watching him sleep.

"There wasn't time, Mother. I found him in the barn. He was ready to collapse from the coughing and lack of breath. I should've called you while Doc Ryan examined him."

"Yes, you should've." She stroked Jasper's brow. He'd laid down within seconds of entering the apartment, falling asleep immediately. "The doctor advised he leave the ranch?"

"Go on an extended vacation. He suggested Seattle, Salt Lake City, or San Diego, but there are other places suitable for people with asthma. The dirt and dust aren't helping Pop."

"Jasper agreed to this?"

"Heck, no." Virgil leaned against the counter in the small kitchen, crossing his arms. "He has to get away from here. You'll go with him, right?"

"Of course." Monica thought of Jasper's plea they renew their marriage vows and how she'd put him off. It had been a mistake.

"Will you remarry, Mother?"

Placing her hand over Jasper's, she looked at her son. "Would you mind asking Nacho if he could prepare us his tortilla soup?"

Shaking his head in frustration, he straightened. She'd deflected his questions each time he'd brought up their marital status. Wyatt had told him to back off and let them figure out their situation, but he hadn't been able to heed his friend's advice.

"Sure. When I bring the soup pot to you, I expect an answer to my question." Leaving before she could respond, his boots pounded the ground on his way to the kitchen.

"He isn't going to stop asking, Monica."

"You're awake. I thought you might be. How long have you been listening?"

"I was never asleep. I'm not ready to leave the ranch."

"What you want isn't going to help your asthma, Jasper. When was the last time you took a vacation?"

Closing his eyes, he pursed his lips. "Can't remember."

"Then it is definitely time."

"There's work to do here. They'll be shorthanded without me, Monica."

"They'll do fine. I understand they've hired a new ranch hand—"

"A woman who worked for a rodeo company," he interrupted.

"Sam grew up on a ranch, handled bucking stock at the rodeos, and is used to hard work. Virgil is doing a great job handling the foreman duties, and Wyatt stepped into Anson's boots without a hiccup. Life is changing, and it's time we changed with it."

Pushing up, he sat alongside Monica on the edge of the bed. "I wouldn't know what to do on a vacation."

"Relaxing would be the most important thing. We should go somewhere you won't be tempted to overdo."

"If I'm not on a ranch, there won't be anything pushing me to overdo."

Chuckling, she stood, placing a hand on his shoulder. "That's what you say now. You're a workaholic, Jasper. My guess is, even on vacation, you'd hunt for things to do."

Staring up at her, he saw the steely determination on her face. He wouldn't fight her on this. Going on vacation for a few weeks wouldn't hurt him, and it would give them time to strengthen their relationship.

"I'll leave the ranch under two conditions."

Narrowing her eyes, she studied him. "What would they be?"

"We renew our vows, and you move in with me."

Chapter Twenty-One

The pounding rain hadn't let up since the last of the guests entered the lodge for lunch. Those looking forward to the challenging hike to the falls had their hopes dashed when Wyatt announced the storm wasn't expected to let up until late afternoon.

"I know this is a huge disappointment for many of you. It is especially hard since this is your last full day at the ranch. There is some good news.

"You all know Gage, who leads the outdoor adventure activities. He has been following the weather. Some of you leave early for your trip home. However, there is a significant number who are with us until the afternoon. Gage has put together a hike to the falls for early tomorrow morning." Wyatt smiled at the cheers erupting around the room. "You'll be back by noon. We'll have boxed lunches prepared, and vans ready for those who require transportation to the airport."

"Where do we sign up?" Wyatt smiled at the guest who spoke up and the others at his table.

"Right here!" Gage raised his hand from a table at the side of the room.

"There you go," Wyatt said. "Sign up before you leave the lodge. Gage and I will stick around to answer questions. And don't forget the excellent desserts Emma has set out."

"Are you planning to go on the hike tomorrow?" Blossom asked Brent while watching Emma place the last of the desserts on the buffet table.

"Unless there's a reason I shouldn't."

"I think it's a great idea. I'll pack while you're gone." Pushing back her chair, Blossom nodded toward the kitchen. "I'm going to see if Emma has time to talk with me."

"Do you want me to go with you?"

Taking his hand, she shook her head. "Thanks, but this is something I need to do on my own."

Standing, Brent kissed her cheek. "Well, I'm going to get dessert, then I'll be in the cabin if you need me."

Watching as he approached the buffet, Blossom fortified herself with several soothing breaths. Even if Emma would allow her to explain, this would not be an easy conversation.

Forcing her feet to move, she headed to the kitchen. Emma stood at one of the large, stainless-steel sinks, rinsing dishes before setting them in one of two commercial washers. Blossom knew almost half of the equipment in the kitchen was new, installed specifically to service the ranch guests. They'd poured a huge amount of money into the new operation. She sincerely hoped it worked out for the Bonners.

"Can I help you?" Nacho's voice had Emma shifting to glance over her shoulder.

"If you can spare her for a few minutes, I'd like to speak with Emma."

Nacho's voice rose to be heard over the noise of one of the commercial dishwashers. "Emma. You got time to speak with one of the guests?"

Turning off the water, Emma dried her hands. She didn't have any idea what Blossom wanted to discuss, and had little time to talk. Seeing no graceful way to get out of it, she took several steps toward her.

"Can we talk in here, or do you want someplace more private?"

"Private would be best." Blossom felt the rock in her stomach grow.

"Let's go to my apartment."

Following Emma toward the back of the lodge, she stepped into a small, yet quaint living room. Furnished in dark woods, deep colored tapestry fabrics, and a leather sofa, Blossom sat down in the chair Emma indicated.

Sitting in a nearby chair, Emma clutched her hands together. "So, what is it you want to talk about?"

Opening her mouth to speak, Blossom closed it, realizing she wasn't as prepared as she first thought. The room was warm, yet she shivered at what had to be said. Tugging the sweater around her neck, she searched for the right words.

"Look, Blossom. I don't have much time. If you'd rather put this off, we can talk later."

"No. This needs to be done now." Licking her lips, she forced herself to look at Emma. "This isn't easy for me, and I'm certain it will be horrible for you to hear."

Emma's stomach lurched at the warning. "You have my attention."

"You remember a few years ago when I called you with news about Trace?"

"How could I forget? My marriage ended because of it."

Blossom lowered her head, staring at the hands clutched in her lap. "I know, and I'll never be able to make up for my part in your divorce."

Throat tight, Emma leaned forward. "Make up for what?"

"What I said about Trace wasn't true. I was paid to tell you the lie."

Stomach heaving, Emma released an anguished cry. "Lied?"

"I'm so sorry."

"Sorry? Your lie ruined my life with Trace, and you're sorry?"

"I don't know what else to say. As much as I want to, I can't go back and undo my actions." Blossom began to rock in the chair, a nervous behavior she'd never been able to conquer. "If it would help, I can talk to Trace."

"Oh, you're going to tell him the truth." Breath coming in short clips, Emma swallowed the bile Blossom's confession caused. "You said someone paid you to lie?"

"Yes."

"Why? Trace was always in the money, but he hadn't achieved the pinnacle until after the divorce. I can't imagine anyone having a grudge against him or me." Emma pursed her lips, trying to conjure up the name of someone who hated them. No one came to mind, except...

"Who paid you?"

"Is it really important to know their identity now? It's been years since your divorce. Wouldn't it be best to let it go?"

Emma gave her a pitying look. "What would you do in my place, Blossom? Would you let it go?"

Closing her eyes, she shook her head. "I suppose not."

"I'll ask again. Who paid you?"

Shoving to her feet, Blossom walked to the window looking out toward the guest cabins and corrals. "I was broke. When she came to me, there was less than fifty cents in my purse and no savings. I'd lost my apartment and was about to lose my car. There was this job, but they weren't hiring for a week. I just needed enough to get through that week."

"Who, Blossom?"

"It was just a hundred dollars."

Emma stared at her, unable to keep the disgust from her features. "You ruined my marriage for a hundred dollars? We didn't have much, but I would've given you money, or at least offered to have you stay with us until the job came through."

Tears Blossom had been working hard to control began streaming down her cheeks. "I understand that now. Back then, I truly believed I had nowhere to turn." Dropping back into the chair, she covered her face with both hands.

"So you took the hundred dollars, obtained the job, and continued with your life?" Reaching out, she picked up a box of tissues, handing it to Blossom.

"Thank you." Dabbing at her face, she wadded up the tissue in her fisted hand.

Lowering her voice, Emma asked once more. "Who paid you?"

Face red, eyes swollen, her mouth twisted into a grimace. "Your mother."

"All right, guys. I think we've done all we can for tonight." Trace surveyed the work he, Jimmy, and Koa completed in the barn. Four stalls needed minor repairs, and another required the sliding metal door be replaced by a new one.

"I'm hungry. Can we have Mom make us something?"

"We already had dinner, son."

"So?"

Jimmy laughed, understanding the young boy's never-ending need for food. "If you're raiding the kitchen, I'm going with you."

"See, Dad. We're both hungry."

Putting away the last of the tools, Trace placed fisted hands on his hips. "All right. But we aren't going to bother your mother. Nacho told me she hadn't left the apartment since after dinner."

He'd walked to the lodge an hour earlier, surprised to find Nacho sitting at a counter drinking coffee and eating a piece of pecan pie. The older man told him Emma left for the apartment right after the last dishes were loaded into the dishwasher.

His first reaction had been to check on her, then reminded himself they weren't together. Something he hoped to change soon.

"If you two are ready, let's see what we can find in the kitchen." Trace led them up the well-worn path from the barn to the lodge, thankful for a break in the rain.

The ranch seemed eerily quiet. Because the bad weather forced them to cancel the usual last night campfire and entertainment, most guests had retreated to their cabins.

Trace hoped Gage was right about the weather clearing before morning. They had fourteen guests confirmed for the hike. The route had been modified to take into account trails that may have been washed out by the storm.

Tomorrow's path was easier, less vertical, but placed them at the same spot to view the falls. Trace would go along, as would Jimmy. Koa could probably handle the trail, but both his parents had vetoed him going.

Entering the kitchen, Trace flipped on lights. There were cookies wrapped and placed on trays, a large bowl of shiny red apples, and bags Nacho would use to pack lunches tomorrow.

"I noticed the light and decided to come check."

Emma traipsed into the kitchen wearing warm sweatpants, heavy sweatshirt, and suede boots with thick, fleece linings. Her swollen, red-rimmed eyes caught Trace's attention, along with the way her mouth sagged downward.

Walking to her, he fought the urge to wrap Emma in his arms. Keeping a foot between them, his gaze roamed her face. "What's wrong?"

"Nothing's wrong."

Giving a slow shake of his head, he touched her arm. "Tell me."

Letting out a tired breath, she shot a look at Koa and Jimmy, both studying the contents of the refrigerator. "There is ham and turkey for sandwiches."

"Thanks, Emma," Jimmy said. "Sound good to you, Koa?"

"Great. Thanks, Mom."

Watching for a moment as they pulled out what they needed, she returned her attention to Trace. "We need to talk."

"Now is a good time. Jimmy, keep an eye on Koa. Emma and I need to talk."

"No problem, Trace. Take your time."

Taking her hand, Trace led the way to her apartment, the only place they'd have privacy. Closing the door, he moved into the living room.

"All right. Talk."

Dropping into one of the upholstered arm chairs, Emma covered her face with both hands. Trace gave her a few minutes before settling in a nearby chair.

"Emma? Tell me what's going on."

Lowering her hands, the misery on her face hit Trace in the gut. "I spoke with Blossom."

"All right."

Forcing herself to take a steadying breath, she met Trace's expectant gaze.

"My mother paid Blossom to tell me you were cheating."

Chapter Twenty-Two

Trace's hands fisted in his lap. He wanted to punch the wall, pounding until his knuckles were red and swollen.

The woman, who'd never tried to hide her dislike for him, had betrayed them. He could see Pauline doing all she could to hurt him. But her daughter? His former mother-in-law would do anything to get what she wanted. Even ruining her daughter's marriage.

Trace believed her need to always be right had contributed to the demise of her second marriage. One morning, Al Bullard rolled out of bed, packed two suitcases and his computer, loaded his truck, and drove away.

He'd given no warning or indicated his discontent with their marriage. Divorce papers were served a few weeks later. Al never spoke to Pauline again, offered no explanation, or apologized.

"You're certain Blossom is telling the truth, Emma?"

"She has no reason to lie."

"I knew Pauline didn't approve of me or our marriage. Paying someone to tell you I was cheating is beyond the actions of a normal person."

Emma opened her mouth to argue, then closed it. Trace was more right than wrong. Her mother's reaction to their marriage had been irrational, as had been the way she treated Trace. Paying Blossom to put the seeds of distrust in Emma's mind wasn't the action of a typical, loving mother.

"We have to confront her," Trace said.

"I'll talk to her."

"No, both of us will speak with her. What she did impacted me in ways I've never mentioned. Her allegations almost lost me my sponsorship money. Without it, I wouldn't have been able to send you the extra money each month."

Lifting a brow, she cocked her head to the side. "Extra money?"

"The extra thousand dollars. I've been sending it in addition to child support since the divorce was final."

"I've never received any extra money, Trace."

Frustrated, he stood, pacing across the room. "The checks were cashed each month, Em."

"Where did you send them?"

"To the same address as the child support. It's a post office box."

"Oh, no." Rising, she joined Trace, taking his hand in hers. "Mother always took care of the child support, depositing it into my checking account. I've never seen any extra money. Mother must have kept it all for herself."

Resting an arm over her shoulders, he kissed her temple. "That's my guess."

"It's hard to accept my mother paid Blossom to lie, and kept the extra money you sent for Koa."

"And you, Em. I already have a college fund established for Koa."

"I don't understand. Where are you getting all this money?"

"I'll tell you all about what I've been doing, but tonight, lets focus on your mother and what we're going to do about her actions."

"She's supposed to leave tomorrow with the friends who brought her to Brilliance. It's too late tonight, and I don't know if there'll be time in the morning. I'll call her to find out." Pulling the phone from her pocket, she called her mother, spoke for a couple minutes, and hung up. A hesitant smile graced her features.

"The schedule has changed. They're leaving Monday. She plans to come out tomorrow, late morning. Are you sure you want to be a part of the conversation?"

Trace closed the distance between them, placing his hands on her shoulders. "Yes. We have the early hike in the morning before the guests leave. The place should be quiet by early afternoon. You let me know when she arrives and I'll meet the two of you here. It's the most private place for our discussion."

She offered a soft snort. "Trust me. If Mother gets upset, her voice rises, and she doesn't care who hears her. Privacy isn't a word I would ever associate with Pauline Bullard."

"We'll have to do our best to keep her calm."

Emma laughed. "She's going to erupt when we confront her about paying Blossom. It will get worse when I ask about your checks. I'm glad the guests will be gone."

He rubbed his eyes with his index finger and thumb. "I should mention this to Wyatt and Virgil so they aren't blindsided if Pauline acts out in front of them." Bending down to press a kiss to her lips, he moved to the apartment door. "I'll send Koa to you. He should be done with his evening snack by now."

The melancholy surprised him. He'd dealt with the loss of his family years ago. At least he believed the morose loneliness, which overcame him every night, had lessened as the days and months passed, leaving him numb as he'd crawl into bed. Now, when there was hope of getting his family back, he still felt an acute sense of isolation.

Sending Koa to the apartment, he stepped outside to a retreating rain. A few light sprinkles dotted his jacket, but the heavy downpour of earlier had vanished.

Trace felt good about tomorrow's hike. He wished he felt the same about Pauline.

Exhilarated after the hike and positive comments from the guests, he headed to the bunkhouse to clean up. His gaze flicked toward the parking lot, landing on Pauline's rental car. A red hot rush of anger at the woman flashed through him, but he quickly tamped it down.

Allowing anger to control his actions had never worked. Not even when Emma announced her intention to divorce had he let anger rule him. Trace wouldn't let it influence him now. Pauline paying Blossom to lie, and the theft of the extra money meant for Emma and Koa, would be dealt with in a calm, rational manner.

Taking a quick shower, he hurried to the lodge, knowing Emma would be busy providing boxed lunches to the guests. Her next job would be preparing light snacks for new guests arriving later in the afternoon. It was a hectic turnaround.

The ranch hired a service to clean the cabins. They swooped in at two o'clock and drove away by four-thirty.

Stepping into the kitchen, he spotted Pauline right away. She sat at a counter, sipping coffee while eating a sandwich and fruit salad. Her eyes widened at the sight of him, face turning a familiar shade of red.

Emma worked close by, sealing the lunch containers before carrying them out to the dining room. Giving Trace a brief smile, she leaned down, speaking close to her mother's ear. When he thought Pauline would respond, she took another bite of her sandwich, fixing her attention on Nacho.

"This one's for you." Emma handed one of the lunches to Trace. "It has an extra sandwich and two bags of chips." She smiled before gathering up the remaining lunches for the last of the departing guests.

A cold chill claimed the kitchen when the door closed behind Emma. Pauline set down her sandwich, slid off the stool, and marched to within a few feet of Trace.

"I'll do everything in my power to keep you and Emma apart," she sputtered, defying him to say otherwise.

Ignoring her, he unwrapped a sandwich, taking a large bite. "What's for dinner, Nacho?"

The cooked speared him a look saying the question was ridiculous. "Same as every Sunday. Meatloaf, mashed potatoes with gravy, and green beans."

"Sounds great. Lemon pie?"

Nacho lifted a brow. "If you stop asking questions and let me work."

Emma swept back into the kitchen, shoving strands of hair from her forehead. "Everyone has their lunch and is now officially on their own."

Pauline marched toward her daughter. "You and I have to talk."

"You're right, Mother. However, Trace will be joining us."

She huffed out a hard breath. "I see no need for that man to be included."

Emma shook her head and walked around Pauline to set the tray she held onto the counter. "I think the apartment is the best place to talk. What do you think, Trace?"

"Fine for me." He shot a look at Nacho, who pretended to ignore their conversation. Trace had a suspicion Emma had given her boss a heads-up on their meeting.

"What we have to discuss is private between you and me, Emma."

"Well, what we have to talk about impacts the three of us...plus Koa. He's playing with a friend, but Trace will be included. Have you finished your lunch?"

Pauline nodded, though her features were rigid with scarcely suppressed rage.

"This shouldn't take too long, Nacho."

"Take whatever time you need, Chica."

"Thank you." She motioned for her mother and Trace to follow her.

Once inside the apartment, she removed the apron, grabbed water for all three, and sat down. "Mother, do you want to start? Be aware, if you're going to repeat all the reasons Trace and I shouldn't be together, don't bother. It's none of your business. The truth is, I never should've listened to you all those years ago."

"Your decision to divorce was a sound one. Don't you recall your conversation with Blossom?"

Emma glanced at Trace, who nodded. "Are you talking about the conversation where you paid Blossom to lie about him?"

Pauline's face paled, mouth pressed into a thin line. Clasping her hands together, her knuckles began turning white.

"I don't know what you're talking about."

"You don't recall giving Blossom a hundred dollars to tell me Trace had cheated?"

Pauline flashed a tormented look at Trace. "He did cheat. Tell her, Trace. For once, tell her the truth."

Any anger he still felt for his former mother-in-law faded to pity. "The truth is, I never cheated on Emma. Never once considered it."

"That's a lie," Pauline shot back.

"Mother!"

Pauline pointed at Trace. "He's lying, Emma." Her mother's harsh assertion quieted the room.

Shifting his gaze to Emma, all Trace could do was give a slow shake of his head. Standing, he paced to the window, looking outside to see Koa playing with another boy. Emma's voice had him turning away.

"Blossom was quite clear that you paid her in cash. She was in a bad place. Broke without a job or place to live. You exploited her situation, bribing Blossom to paint Trace as a cheating husband. What I don't understand is why?"

Pauline shifted in the overstuffed chair. Face an unpleasant shade of gray, she grabbed a tissue from her pocket, dabbing at her eyes. Emma had seen this play for sympathy before. Her mother was a master manipulator, playing people against each other while seeking their pity. This time, she'd gone too far.

"Mother, we know you gave Blossom money to lie. Please, tell us why."

Chapter Twenty-Three

Hands resting on the arms of the chair, Pauline's fingers dug into the thick, tapestry fabric. She didn't lift her head to meet Emma and Trace's expectant gazes.

"Mother?"

Glassy eyes stared straight ahead, as if looking into the past. "He was a rodeo cowboy."

"Who?"

"Your father."

Emma leaned forward. "My father wasn't a rodeo cowboy. You told me he was a traveling salesman who died in a car crash after I was born."

Pauline punched out a mirthless chuckle. "Is that what I said?"

"Yes. More than once. You said he left us nothing."

"That part was true. He didn't leave us a dime."

"But he wasn't a salesman?"

"He was a rodeo cowboy. Married me at eighteen. It was exciting for a while, then I got pregnant." Pauline focused on Emma with a start, as if realizing there were others in the room.

"What happened while you were pregnant?" Trace spoke in a calm, low voice.

"He moved us from rodeo to rodeo, provided a trailer and food, but almost never came home at night. The man was a real scoundrel, the same as all rodeo cowboys. He stuck around until your second birthday. One day, he moved on to the next rodeo, but left us behind. I never saw him again."

Emma fought to draw a breath. Placing a hand on her chest, she swallowed, unable to speak.

Alarmed, Trace knelt beside her. "Are you all right, Emma?" He rubbed her back, moving his hand in slow circles.

"I'll be fine. It's just not what I expected to hear. All these years..."

Irritated at the pain her mother caused, he looked at Pauline. "Why did you tell Emma her father was a salesman who died?"

She shifted her gaze slowly toward Trace. "Because I didn't want her to know that he was a lowlife cowboy."

"Most of those in the rodeo are honest, good people. They work hard and love their families."

She shook her head. "I don't believe you."

"You had a horrible experience with one man, Pauline, and I'm sorry for that. But lying about me, and paying Blossom, was wrong on every level. Can you understand that?"

Pauline's blank eyes met his. "Understand?"

"What your lies have cost Emma, Koa, and me. No matter our troubles, we were a family."

Emma swiped away a tear, still reeling from the information about her father. She had so many questions, knowing today wasn't the time to ask. They had another issue to discuss with her mother. After the disclosure about her father, Emma wished the second conversation could be put off.

To Emma's surprise, her mother covered her face with both hands and sobbed. In all her years growing up, she'd never seen her cry.

When Pauline's body began to shake, Emma moved to console her. Trace held her back with a hand on her arm.

"Let her get it out, sweetheart. She's been holding it in for a long time."

Instead of going to her mother, Emma grabbed a box of tissues. "Here, Mother." Setting it down, she returned to her chair and waited with Trace.

Several minutes ticked by before Pauline grabbed a tissue, then a few more. Picking up her bottle of water, she drank half before recapping it.

"Now you know about your real father. Maybe I should have told you the truth, but I didn't."

Emma's voice quivered. "He never did contact you to find out how we were doing?"

"Never. The man treated us as if we didn't exist."

"Did you ever learn what happened to him?" Emma asked. "I mean, is he still alive?"

"I have no idea and don't care. I'm sorry if that sounds harsh, but he left us with no money, and only the food left in the trailer. You were too young to remember, Emma. I found a job working for a fast food company during the day and cleaning vacated apartments. A friend would take care of you when I worked. She wouldn't take money, but loved the fast food I brought home each day." Dabbing at her eyes, Pauline fell silent.

Trace held Emma's hand as they walked under the darkening sky. Their conversation with Pauline had been more intense and revealing than either of them had expected.

Leaning down, Trace brushed a kiss across Emma's lips. They no longer worried about anyone learning of their desire to rekindle their relationship.

"I'm not sure Mother understands the damage she caused by paying Blossom to lie."

Trace squeezed her hand. "It was always her intention to drive us apart."

"And she succeeded."

"Yes." Trace guided them to the largest corral holding several horses. "I don't believe she feels any regret at the pain her actions caused. That bothers me, Em."

"I know. It bothers me too. Especially when she's around Koa. I'll wonder what she's telling him."

"Maybe it would be best to limit the time they spend together. Just don't make Koa available for a while." He stopped at the corral fence, placing a booted foot on the lowest rung.

"We still need to talk to her about the money you sent. I'm not sure now is the time." Emma leaned against his side. "I've learned so much about Mother in the last two days. None of it good."

"Pauline did the best she could under difficult circumstances. She worked two jobs and found a solid person to take care of you."

"But she lied about my real father. All these years, I thought the man died, when he could still be alive. I understand the pain she suffered. Still, she shouldn't have lied to me."

"You're right. Are you interested in trying to find him?"

"My father? I don't know. He never showed any interest in me, so it could be a huge waste of time. I'd rather go forward and not dwell on the past."

Trace opened his mouth to reply, hesitating when his phone vibrated. Checking the caller I.D. he shook his head. "Sorry, but I have to take this call."

Walking several feet away, he turned his back to Emma. "Hey, Augie. What's going on?"

"It's your father. He's been rushed to the hospital."

"I'm sorry, Wyatt, but I have to be there for my father."

"Don't worry about it, Trace. Take whatever time you need." Wyatt glanced at Virgil, who nodded in agreement. "Sam is turning out to be a real good hire. Between her and the others, we will be fine."

"I don't know how long I'll be gone. Could be a few days or weeks." Trace scrubbed a hand over his face, worry etched in the lines around his eyes and mouth.

"Keep us posted, and don't worry about things around here. Focus on your family." Wyatt walked around the desk, extending his hand. "We'll be praying for his full recovery."

"Thanks." Trace shook Wyatt's hand, then Virgil's, before heading out. His truck was already packed. Now he had to face Emma. He'd told her little, other than his father had another heart attack. This one worse than the first attack a few months earlier.

Trace had hoped over the next few days to explain about his ownership of the family ranch, and his purchase of Folton Rodeo Stock. Emma didn't know the full extent of his success as a rodeo competitor, nor how he'd invested the money, tripling the value over the years.

As a nationally ranked contender, he'd made real good money, but not nearly as much as what his sponsors paid. Between the two, he'd become one of the highest paid rodeo cowboys on the circuit.

Those discussions would have to wait until he returned. And if his father didn't recover? Trace didn't want to consider that possibility.

"Dad! Dad, wait!" Koa ran to him, breathing hard, his eyes wild. "I want to come with you."

"Ah, buddy, this isn't a good time for you to ride along. Grandpa is very sick, and I'll be at the hospital."

"I can stay with Grandma."

"She'll be at the hospital too."

"I'm a hard worker. I can help at the ranch while you're gone."

"It's just not the right time, Koa."

"Trace. Could I speak to you?" Emma stood a few feet away. "It won't take long."

"Hang on, Koa, while I speak to your mama."

Bottom lip jutting out, he nodded. "Ooookay."

Taking Emma's hand, he guided them several feet away. "What do you need to tell me?"

"I know this may seem an odd request, but would it be all right if Koa went with you?"

Blinking, he glanced behind him at his son, then returned his attention to Emma. "You want me to take him?"

"Well, if it isn't too much trouble. I mean, Koa will do whatever you ask, and would love to see the ranch. I know you and your mother won't be there much, but maybe there's a ranch hand who can keep an eye on him when you're at the hospital."

Rubbing his jaw, he considered the pros and cons. Then a light went off in his head. "You're asking this to get him away from Pauline, right?"

"That's part of it. Most of it is him being able to spend time with his father. He'll also get to be around his grandma."

"I know Mom would love it, but her attention will be on Dad. To be honest, my focus will be on him too." Removing his hat, he ran a sleeve over his damp forehead, then slapped it against his leg. "What the heck. Pack what he needs, along with snacks so I don't have to stop, and I'll take him."

Emma touched his arm. "Are you sure?"

"Yeah. We'll spend time together, and I know Mom will be thrilled." Whirling around, he strode back to Koa. "All right, son. You'll be going with me."

"Yea!" He jumped up and down, clapping his hands.

"Go help your mother get packed."

"Okay!"

"Don't forget, you'll be doing a lot of work while you're at the ranch."

"I know! Can I pack now?"

Chuckling, Trace ruffled Koa's hair. "Yeah. Go on."

Watching his son run after Emma brought a bit of relief to his aching heart. Trace didn't know what his mother would do without her husband. He didn't know what he'd do without the man who'd guided him through life.

It was going on eight o'clock on a dark night, with a solid five-hour drive ahead of them. At least it wasn't winter. After the initial excitement wore off, Koa would no doubt sleep through most of the drive. It would give Trace time to think.

Think about his father, his ranch, buying the rodeo stock company, and his relationship with Emma. A relationship he planned to make permanent real soon.

Chapter Twenty-Four

"What in the world?"

"I brought Koa with me, Mom." Trace carried his sleeping son into the house and to the bedroom next to his. "He slept most of the way. I'm surprised you're still up."

Audrey Griffin folded back the blankets and sheets, fluffing the pillow. "He's gotten so big." Her voice held a strong dose of regret at not seeing her grandson for so long.

Putting his arm around his mother, he gave her a squeeze. "I know, Mom. That's why Koa coming with me was important. He'll be a big help around here."

"I'm sure he will be." She couldn't take her gaze off Koa. "You and Emma must be getting along pretty well if she let you bring him to the ranch."

"I'll tell you all about it tomorrow. Tonight, I want to hear about Dad."

"Probably won't sleep tonight, so I'll make coffee. Are you hungry? I can make an early breakfast."

"Don't go to any trouble, Mom."

"No trouble. I'm going to fix eggs and hashbrowns for me."

Trace grinned. "Add bacon to mine and we're set." He watched her continue to stare at Koa before putting an around her and guiding her downstairs.

"What's my grandson like?" Audrey pulled out two cast iron skillets, starting bacon in one and hashbrowns in the other.

"I hate to tell you this, but he's just like me when I was his age."

Stirring the bacon, she looked at him, one brow lifted. "A hellion, huh?"

It took Trace a bit before figuring out his mother was trying to get her mind off his father. She'd always been a strong woman. Still, people could only deal with so much. Bringing Koa had been a brilliant idea. He'd have to call Emma and let her know.

"Active, Mom. He can tack up his own horse, ride, rope, work cattle drives, and my personal favorite, muck the stalls. The boy never complains. Work or play, he has the same amount of enthusiasm."

"I'm sure he's wonderful, Trace." She hid the threatening tears by turning back to the stove. Plating the food, she set Trace's breakfast in front of him before taking her own seat. He waited a few minutes before asking about his father.

"Coop's still in intensive care. They'll know more in a couple days. I'll be heading back to the hospital when I'm finished eating."

"You need your rest, Mom. I'll go to the hospital and sit with Dad."

Having little appetite, she gave up on the food and set down her fork. "I'd never be able to sleep. What if he wakes up and looks for me? Coop gets agitated when I'm not there for him."

A strong, robust rancher with a rich, deep voice, Cooper Griffin had always commanded attention from everyone. Most respected him, others feared him. At least that's what Trace remembered before his father's first heart attack. The changes had been profound.

The most important person, and constant in his life, was Audrey Griffin, the petite woman who was the true ruler of the ranch. Her five-foot-four height never mattered to the six-foot-two rancher. The same as Cooper, no one messed with Audrey, including their children.

"If that's what you want, Mom. I'll join you after getting Koa settled."

"Bring him to the hospital. I'm certain your father would want to see him."

"If you're sure."

Audrey reached over to pat his arm. "I am. When you return to the ranch, you should meet with Augie. A lot has happened in the last two weeks."

"I haven't heard anything from Augie."

Audrey's mouth twisted in frustration. "Because Coop told him not to bother you. Foolish old man thought he could help out and take some of the load off you."

"Tell me what happened, Mom."

"Robber Folton tried to renege on his deal to sell the stock business. Said he rethought it all and wanted more money. Coop knew the deal was ironclad, no way for Robber to walk away from it without incurring big legal fees. He set up a meeting with Robber and brought our attorney.”

“Is that when Dad had the heart attack?” Trace gripped the cup of coffee tight enough to turn his knuckles white.

“No, it was afterward. Robber backed down, but convinced Hal and Bitsy to change their minds about staying. They agreed to two weeks from closing the deal to train replacements, then they’re heading out of the area.”

“Two weeks, huh?”

“It’s for the best, Trace. They aren’t bad people, but their loyalty would always be with Robber. I have no doubt they would’ve fed him information about how you were doing.”

“I’d better get the word out about needing replacements for them.”

“I’ve already talked to a number of people. Augie and I met with several.” Shoving the chair back, she walked to the counter with an older black telephone. Audrey picked up a pad of lined yellow paper, handing it to Trace. “Considering just those on this list, the first two names are my favorites. They’re married, the same as Hal and Bitsy. In their thirties. Both worked for the same rodeo promotion company and understand the process of stock bidding. The other four on the list are good possibles, and you may want to talk to all of them. Well, I’m going to freshen up before driving to the hospital.”

Trace studied the list. His mother had made copious notes, which included Augie's comments. She had good instincts. If she thought the husband and wife were a good fit, then he'd meet with them first.

Heading to his bedroom, he sat on the side of the bed. Deciding a couple hours sleep would do him a lot of good, he didn't bother setting the alarm before stretching out and closing his eyes.

"You let him take my grandson? What were you thinking?" Pauline crossed her arms.

"Koa is Trace's son too. Both of us decided taking him to the ranch was a good idea. Audrey and Cooper haven't seen their grandson in much too long." Emma removed eggs, onions, yellow bell peppers, mushrooms, ham, and cheese from the refrigerator.

She'd waited until the new slate of guests ate their breakfast before fixing something for them. Putting off their meal also assured her Nacho would be taking a break before they tackled lunch.

"That's their own fault. They could've driven down here to see him."

Lifting a bowl from the cabinet, Emma began assembling the ingredients for omelets, working to contain her irritation. Her mother had been complaining since first learning Koa had left Whistle Rock Ranch with Trace.

"How many times have you visited, Mother?"

"That's different. I didn't want to drive alone."

"Cooper and Audrey had good reasons, also." Emma knew part of the reason was she hadn't made much of an effort to stay in touch with them. She'd sent Christmas cards and pictures of Koa instead of taking the time to visit.

Audrey and Cooper had always been good to her and Koa. The divorce hadn't changed their concern or love.

"Well, I don't like it. Afterall, you and Trace are divorced, and he's made little effort to see his son."

"Most of that was me pushing him away. He called at least twice a week to speak with Koa, and always asked if he could visit. I made excuses each time." Emma now dealt with the guilt.

"You did the right thing."

"No, Mother, I didn't. Trace deserved better. Knowing you paid Blossom to lie makes my actions worse. I don't believe you understand what you did was wrong."

Pauline didn't respond, though her shoulders sagged.

"We're working on our relationship, and I expect you to stay quiet. No interference. Can you do that for me?"

"You're making a mistake."

"Can you stay out of our lives, Mother?"

"Fine. I'll leave my opinions to myself."

Emma wasn't sure she believed Pauline could stick to their agreement, but kept her concerns to herself. There was another issue they needed to discuss.

Finishing their omelets, she decided there was no better time than now to tackle the subject weighing on her.

She suspected Trace planned to be a part of the discussion. With her mother leaving tomorrow, Emma felt obligated to deal with the missing money before Pauline left.

"Trace asked me about the additional money he's been sending me, Mother." Emma saw the slightest change in Pauline's features. "I told him I'd never seen any additions to my checking account. Do you know anything about this?"

"No, I don't."

"He's been sending the extra money to your address for quite a while. Are you certain you haven't seen the checks?"

"I don't remember any additional money from Trace. Maybe he's not telling you the truth."

Emma rested her arms on the table, leaning toward her mother. "I know you cashed the checks. Your signature is on the back of each one. What did you do with the money?"

Pauline's jaw tightened as a flush crept up her face. Her mouth opened, then slammed shut.

"This is important. Trace sent the checks, in addition to the amount we agreed on during the divorce, for anything out of the ordinary Koa needed. They were mailed out to you, as he didn't have my address. You signed my name on the back in order to cash them. I want the money back."

Face falling, Pauline covered her face with both hands. "I don't have it."

"What does that mean?"

Dropping her hands exposed red rimmed eyes and a grim expression. "I didn't think you and Trace would ever consider getting back together."

"So you felt free to steal the money?"

"It wasn't stealing."

Emma leaned back, crossing her arms. "What would you call it?"

"Well, not stealing. I had needs."

Chest squeezing, Emma closed her eyes as she began to understand her mother's meaning. "You received a generous settlement from your divorce, plus the house, and all the personal property. Including your car."

"I never liked the furniture."

Ignoring the desire to scream, Emma took several soothing breaths. "You're telling me you spent all the money Trace sent for Koa on new furniture?"

"Not all of it. Some I used to update the kitchen. Nothing major. Some new lighting, a different faucet for the sink...well, I don't remember everything."

Emma couldn't form a response. All the money Trace had sent for Koa went toward sprucing up her mother's home. "What you did was unconscionable. I should file charges against you, Mother. Instead, I want you to repay every dollar, even if you have to sell your car."

"I can't do that. How would I get around?"

"Friends, neighbors, or call a cab. Or take the money out of your savings."

"But that's for an emergency."

Hearing Nacho emerge from the back, Emma lowered her voice. "Trust me, Mother. Either you repay the missing money within the week, or I will call an attorney."

Chapter Twenty-Five

Emma hated threatening her mother. Knowing Pauline well, she understood nothing else would motivate her to repay the money.

Her mother had left with her friends the following day and was now back home. Hopefully, she had started the process to make good on the debt.

What Emma had learned about her mother stunned as much as hurt her. She still had a hard time believing what Pauline had done. The extent of her betrayal.

Emma knew she had to stay strong in her threat. If she wavered at all, her mother would take advantage. Pulling out her phone, she texted Trace.

"How much money did you send for Koa?"

A few minutes passed before he responded with a number. Sucking in a breath, Emma realized why her mother's face had turned a reddish purple color when given a week to replace the money. The sum was much larger than Emma imagined. She forced herself to shove all of it away.

Today would be a day of celebration. Jasper and Monica had announced they planned to renew their vows before leaving for Hawaii. Everyone on the ranch, including the guests, were invited to the ceremony, as well as the reception afterward.

Nacho made special sheet cakes using three large pans. They would be served after a bountiful buffet of roast beef, ham, turkey, three kinds of potatoes, and several salad choices.

Emma was glad for the diversion. She missed Koa and Trace, especially at night when alone in her apartment. Last night, it occurred to her she'd never lived alone. She went from her mother's house to a home shared with Trace. Then Koa had been born, almost guaranteeing she wouldn't be alone for at least eighteen years. She'd be glad when the two men in her life returned.

That final thought had stayed with her. Did she and Trace have the possibility of a second chance? Is that what she wanted? The answers to both was a decisive yes.

"Emma. Please check on the turkey and ham. They should be heated through by now. Also the au gratin potatoes. Keep them all warm until they're served after the ceremony. I'm supposed to remind you that Jasper and Monica expect us to attend the ceremony."

"You go, Nacho. One of us has to stay in the kitchen to make certain nothing overcooks."

"No, you should be the one to go. I don't like attending those social things, and Jasper knows it. You'll have a much better time than I would."

"If you're certain."

"I am." Nacho wiped his hands down his apron. "Go ahead and get ready."

Emma loosened her apron, looking down at the top and jeans she wore. Her usual attire while working. "This will have to do. Besides, I don't have much else."

Emma joined the other guests fifteen minutes later, glad she hadn't changed. Everyone, except Jasper and Monica, were dressed in casual clothes, many in jeans and western shirts.

Watching the ceremony, her eyes teared. She'd never watched a couple renew their vows. Similar to wedding vows, she found it moving to watch a couple, so obviously in love, declare their feelings after so many years.

Afterward, she congratulated the couple, spoke with a few friends, and started back to the lodge when a deep voice caught her attention. Turning, she saw a tall, older man, with deep grooves in his face and a notable limp, talking with Wyatt.

Emma was sure she'd never met him, yet something seemed familiar. She inched closer, hoping to hear a little of their conversation.

"We already have a foreman. You'd be a ranch hand, working alongside the others. If that appeals to you, then there's plenty of work."

"Being a ranch hand is fine with me. I can start today."

She saw Wyatt study him before a smile crossed his face. He spotted Virgil, waving him over. "Virgil, this is

Rance Nelson. He's our newest ranch hand. A former rodeo competitor."

Rance Nelson. Emma thought she'd heard the name before. Wyatt mentioned he'd been on the rodeo circuit. Maybe Trace had spoken of him.

Emma didn't have time to figure it out now. She had to get back to the kitchen to help Nacho set out the food.

"How you feeling today, Dad?" Trace entered the private room with Koa. Grandfather and grandson had hit it off at their first meeting, and Koa insisted on visiting each day.

"How do you think? Ah, there's my grandson. Come over here and tell me what you've been doing." Cooper motioned with his hand to a spot next to the bed. Koa started talking before he reached his grandfather's side.

"I learned to use little leather straps for attaching reins and stuff, Grandpa."

"That's an important skill."

"Yeah. Augie said I'd use it a lot."

Cooper winked at his son, who stood a few feet away. "He's right. You can't go wrong listening to Augie."

"That's what he said, Grandpa."

Trace tried to suppress a laugh. Cooper didn't see the need. He let out a loud guffaw.

"No one ever said Augie lacked self-confidence. What else did you learn?"

"Grandma taught me how to make the beef stew you like. She said you'd want it when you get home."

"Your grandma is a real smart woman, Koa."

"Dad told me that already. Oh, and she taught me how to make biscuits." Koa's face scrunched up. "That wasn't as much fun."

Chuckling, Cooper gave a sober nod. "I wouldn't think so."

"I told Grandma I wanted to learn how to make banana bread the same as hers. She toasts it and spreads butter on it."

"I remember. You be sure and save some for me."

Koa nodded at his grandfather. "I will. Augie picked out a horse for me to ride when I'm visiting. He's kind of old, but better than nothing."

This had the men chuckling again before Cooper closed his eyes for a bit. "Come on, Koa. We should let Grandpa rest."

"I'm all right," Cooper murmured, forcing his eyes open. They fought him, closing a few seconds later. Not long afterward, he began to snore.

Placing both hands over his mouth, Koa tried to contain his laugh.

"Time for us to head home, buddy."

"Okay." Koa cast one more glance at his grandfather. "Can we stop for ice cream?"

"Sure can."

"Is Trace around?" A tall lanky cowboy stood with his arms hanging loose by his sides.

Augie looked him up and down while chewing on the large wad of bubble gum. "Who wants to know?"

The younger man held out his hand. "Jake Kelman. I'm a friend of Trace's."

Accepting the hand, Augie looked toward the house. "He's inside doing paperwork. You looking for a job?"

"Might be. Depends on what's going on."

"Picky, huh? Guess I don't blame you." Augie waved his hand. "Enter through the back door." Turning away, he walked into the barn.

Watching his retreat, Jake let out a deep breath before heading to the house. Knocking first, he opened the back door. He glanced around at the kitchen he'd been in at least a hundred times.

"Trace?"

Heavy boots pounded on the hardwood floor before Trace appeared. "Hey, Jake. Where the heck have you been?"

"Long story. I called Whistle Rock Ranch and the cook said you'd gone home to help with your father. What's going on with Coop?"

Trace motioned to a chair on his way to the counter. "Coffee?"

"Yeah, thanks."

"Dad had another heart attack. The second in less than six months. I'm hoping they'll let him come home soon. Mom's with him." Handing a cup of black coffee to Jake, Trace sat down with his own.

"How's she doing?" He blew across the hot liquid before taking a sip.

"Tired. Pushing herself too hard. If she keeps it up, she may end up sick."

Jake gave a slow nod, taking another swallow of coffee. "Do you remember when my dad had cancer?"

"Of course. He isn't having a relapse, is he?"

"No. What I meant was that Mom hardly ate or slept. I offered to hire someone, but she wouldn't hear of it. She ended up sick. Took a few months to recover her strength. I left the last half of the rodeo season to take care of both of them. The difference was, I hired a nurse to help out. You may want to consider the same."

Trace stared into his cup. "I've mentioned it to Mom, but so far, she's not warming to the idea."

"Wants to do it all herself. Nothing new there."

Chuckling without a bit of humor, Trace sipped his cooling coffee. "Yeah. So, what are you doing here?"

"That's the long story I mentioned earlier. An issue came up with my former girlfriend."

"Which one? I haven't kept track."

Jake's lips tipped upward. "No reason you should. This was Jill. You remember her. Long, dark brown hair, almost as tall as me, and skinny. Too skinny."

"Always flirting with your friends."

"Yep, that's her. We lasted about two months before it ended."

"Your choice?"

"You know it." He finished his coffee, setting the cup aside. "She got herself into some trouble and wanted my help." Jake shrugged, as if it was a given he'd help her. "Jill showed up at my place. Her current boyfriend had roughed her up pretty good. No broken bones, but you know how I feel about violence against a woman."

"It's not all right under any circumstances." Trace felt the same.

The two had talked about it several times growing up when a guy they knew beat up his girlfriend. More than once, one or both of them had a *discussion* with the guy. It was rare the talk had to be repeated.

"I took her to the family doctor, who took X-rays and got her patched up. The boyfriend found out she was staying with me and made some threats. We got in each other's face. I told him how it would be if he ever laid a hand on her again. Last I heard, he'd moved back home to Michigan. Sorry I didn't call you sooner, but it was a little hectic."

"What's your plan now?"

Jake scratched the back of his neck. "Came for your advice. I wouldn't turn down a job here, but I'm curious about Whistle Rock Ranch."

"You can start here today. The thing is, Whistle Rock may be a good fit for you."

Jake leaned forward, resting his arms on the table. "How so?"

A fleeting smile crossed Trace's face. "Well, I have this plan..."

Chapter Twenty-Six

The back door slammed opened as Koa ran into the kitchen. He froze at the look on Trace's face. "Sorry."

"You do that when your grandma is home and you'll be mucking stalls until we leave."

The grimace on Koa's face signaled his understanding. "Sorry," he repeated. His attention moved to the man at the table with his father.

"Koa, this is Jake."

Standing, Jake held out his hand. "Hey there, Koa."

He placed his small hand in Jake's much larger one. "Hi."

"You've grown up since I last saw you. I guess you were about four."

"I'm nine now."

Sitting back down, he grinned. "I'll bet you can do just about anything around the ranch."

Returning the smile, Koa's chest puffed out a little. "Almost. Augie and Dad are teaching me."

Trace stood, taking the two empty cups to the sink. "I'm sure Grandpa will add his thoughts when he gets home."

"Dad, I have to talk to you."

"Well...go ahead."

Koa looked unsure for a moment, then shrugged. "The boy at the ranch next door invited me for dinner. Can I go?"

Trace thought a moment, trying to recall who owned the ranch next to theirs. "What's his name?"

"Tommy."

"Do you know his last name?"

Koa shook his head. "No. They're new here too. Can I go?"

A knock on the back door preceded Augie joining them. "The kid is Tommy Russel. His dad is Cody Russell. Says he knows you. He's outside with Tommy."

A huge smile appeared on Trace's face. "Geez. I haven't seen Cody in years. He's living next door? You remember him, Jake. He was on the circuit for a while."

Without another word, Trace followed Augie outside. Right behind him were Koa and Jake.

"Cody Russell." Trace pulled him into a bro hug. "How are you, man?"

"Doing great."

"You remember Jake Kelman?"

"Sure do." He extended his hand. "Good to see you, Jake."

"Same here."

Cody set his hand on the shoulder of a boy about Koa's age. "This is my son, Tommy."

They greeted Tommy before Trace turned to Koa. "Why don't you take Tommy to see your horse?"

"Okay. Come on, Tommy." The two ran off, Augie lifting a hand to signal he'd keep watch on them.

"Come inside and tell us what's going on with you, Cody."

Coffee in front of them, Cody described his rodeo ending injury, forcing him to pull back from competing. "My family and I are living at my uncle's place next door. He bought the ranch a few months ago with his retirement money. I'm his only ranch hand, but the truth is, he can't afford to pay me. We get room and board. My wife is a CPA, works at an accounting firm in town. She and I trade off making meals, doing laundry, and cleaning the house. Penny was a couple years behind us in high school. She competed in barrel racing and breakaway roping."

Something clicked in Trace's head. Reaching into a pocket, he pulled out the list his mother prepared for him about replacements for Hal and Bitsy. His gaze landed on Penny Russell's name.

"You applied for the job at Folton Rodeo Stock."

Cody stared at his cup a moment, his face coloring. "Yeah. I wasn't going to bring it up."

"Why not? You and Penny have some great experience."

"It didn't seem right to hit you up for a job so soon."

Trace read his mother's notes, a slow grin appearing. "When can you start?"

Eyes widening, Cody's jaw dropped. "Are you sure? I intend to—"

Trace held up a hand. "I don't have a lot of time to make decisions. This one is easy. You and Penny can take over the work being done by Hal and Bitsy when the deal closes.

They'll stay for two weeks to train you. Mom already gave you the salaries." Trace set the paper on the table. "Do you want the jobs?"

"Yes, we do."

"Great. I know you'll need to work the schedule out with your uncle, and Penny will have to give notice."

"My uncle will be good with me working a few hours a week at his place. Penny can give notice anytime." Cody's eyes flashed in amusement. "Her father owns the firm."

"If the deal closes this week, you'll need to be ready to train on Monday. Is that workable?"

"Absolutely. Whatever date you need us, we'll be ready."

Emma laid in bed after several long days in the kitchen, her back aching as much as her feet. She'd taken on extra work, allowing Nacho some well-earned time off.

The number of guests this week had trailed off from the previous three, yet her exhaustion was real. Emma believed her additional fatigue was due to her mother's visit.

Something else also weighed on her. Tossing off the covers, she slid into a flannel shirt before starting her laptop. Searching the certified records for her birth state, Emma completed the required form, selected expedited delivery, paid the fee, and placed the order.

The easiest solution would've been to ask her mother for the birth certificate. With the tension between them, Emma didn't have the energy to go through a prolonged inquisition of the reason for requesting it. Nothing was ever easy with her mother.

Slipping under the covers, she again tried to fall asleep. Images of Trace and Koa slid across her mind. Emma missed them both, and wished she'd been able to go with them. She hadn't heard from either in two days, making a mental note to call in the morning. Sending up a short prayer Cooper was recovering, Emma closed her eyes a final time before drifting off to sleep.

Emma's phone rang, waking her at six o'clock. She should've been up and in the kitchen an hour ago. Scrambling out of bed, she saw the image of Trace, she smiled.

"Hey."

"Hey, beautiful. Am I interrupting your work?"

Securing the phone between her ear and shoulder, she shoved her legs into the jeans folded on a chair. "Not at all. You woke me up, which is good."

"Bad night?"

"Sort of."

"Do you want to talk about it?"

She thought about it, knowing there wasn't time. "I can't now. Maybe later?"

"Anytime, sweetheart."

Tying the laces on her work shoes, she straightened. "Did you call for a reason?"

"I do have some positive things to tell you, but they'll wait for later. How about I call you after lunch?"

"Great. After two would be best."

"Will do. Love you, Em."

"Love you too." Ending the call, she felt a twist of anxiety pass through her.

Emma did love Trace and wanted a second chance. Yet she still harbored a small amount of hesitation about allowing herself to fully trust her emotions. Now wasn't the time to sort it all out.

Rushing to the kitchen, she came face-to-face with the new ranch hand. Rance Nelson held a cup of coffee while eating a piece of toast.

"Ma'am." He moved out of her way, though his gaze never left hers.

Her throat tightened as a ripple of recognition struck her. It made no sense. She'd met the man for the first time at the reception for Jasper and Monica.

"Good morning, Mr. Nelson. How are you doing?"

"Real fine. I get up early, and thought I'd try to talk Nacho into an early breakfast."

"Here you go." Nacho set a plate of eggs, bacon, and potatoes in front of him. "Do you want this every morning?"

"If it's not too much trouble." Rance picked up the plate, setting it on the counter by the window.

"Breakfasts are the easiest meal. It shouldn't be a problem." Nacho grabbed a tub of butter from the refrigerator. "Emma, can you start the bacon and sausage?"

She stood in front of the inside grill with packages of the meats in front of her. "Already on it."

Nacho looked at Rance. "Emma is the best. Someday, she'll be taking over for me."

Rance lifted a brow. "That right?" He scooped up another forkful of eggs.

"Yep. She can do it all now, but I'm not ready to give up."

Taking a bite of bacon, he chewed, swallowing before he spoke. "I hear you. Can't do what I used to, but I'm not the type to sit in a rocking chair and talk about the past." His expression turned dark before he looked back down at his plate. "You got kids, Nacho?"

"Nope. I've got an older brother south of Tucson. He's got a large place with extra bedrooms. I'll go there. You have kids?"

Rance hesitated a moment. "A daughter somewhere."

Emma's stomach clenched. Again, her reaction made no sense. Lots of men were estranged from their children.

Finishing the last bite of potatoes, Rance took his plate to the sink. "Real good, Nacho. Thanks."

He didn't look up from where he prepared slices of pumpkin bread for the guests. "No problem. See you tomorrow morning."

Rance set his hat back on his head, touching the brim. "Nice seeing you again, Emma. And call me Rance."

She smiled, though it faded when he turned to leave. Watching him through the window, she still felt a pinch of recognition.

Emma recalled her mother saying her father left right after her second birthday. He'd moved on to another rodeo, not taking them with him. Why had he stuck around that long if he planned to leave? Had he ever tried to find her? Was he still alive? If so, where was he?

She had so many questions. Emma could ask her mother. Regrettably, she didn't trust the answers Pauline would provide.

Turning the bacon on the large grill, she wondered how long it would be before she could trust her mother again. Had lying become the norm in Pauline's world?

Placing the cooked meat on a tray under the warming lights, she thought of Trace. Something more was going on with him. He'd always talked of going home to help his parents after leaving the rodeo.

Traveling to Whistle Rock Ranch for a cowhand job didn't make sense. Unless it was done to get closer to her and Koa, which is what Emma believed. What had he left behind to take the job?

Chapter Twenty-Seven

"Can I get you anything else, Dad?" Trace stepped back from the bed after slipping another pillow behind his father.

"I'm fine. Stop fussing over me. You and your mother are going to make me wish I was back at the hospital."

Trace grinned. "Not likely. You don't have a call button, so just yell if you need anything. Mom should be here with bottles of water in a few minutes."

"Don't you go running off. I want to hear about the Folton deal, and anything that's gone on since the heart attack."

Trace had avoided topics dealing with the ranch while his father was in the hospital, not wanting to add further stress. Cooper had three stents added to the two inserted after his first heart attack. The cardiologist had given his father a warning before signing the release.

"Cut out as much red meat, cheese, eggs, and rich foods, such as gravy and dessert, as possible. Substitute with fish, turkey, and chicken, plus lots of vegetables and fruit."

On the way home, Cooper had torn up the suggested diet, smiling to himself. The smile faded when Audrey pulled out a copy from her purse, waving the paper in front of him. Koa had laughed at the deep groan from his grandfather.

Sitting in one of the two overstuffed chairs, Trace leaned forward, resting his arms on his legs.

"Robber gave up trying to stop the sale."

"I already knew about that."

Trace sat back, crossing one leg over the other at the ankles. "Did you know Hal and Bitsy decided not to stay?"

"What?" Cooper growled. "They assured me they'd stay."

"Robber must've talked them out of staying. Doesn't matter, Dad. I already hired another couple as their replacements."

He told them about Cody and Penny, reminding Cooper he and Cody were friends from school. His father's only response was they were too inexperienced. After Trace explained more of their background, Cooper grunted and let it go.

"What are you going to do about your job at Whistle Rock?" Cooper knew Anson Bonner, had heard the man also suffered a heart attack. He'd retired. Cooper had no intention of doing the same.

"I have that covered. It's the perfect job for Jake. When Koa and I head back, he's coming with us. Given Jake's experience, Wyatt and Virgil won't have an issue."

Trace studied his father's face, seeing his eyes close, open, then close again. "I'm going to let you sleep." Other than a shaky snore, Cooper didn't respond.

Closing the bedroom door behind him, he pulled out his phone. He and Emma had spoken each of the last few days, neither doing more than asking after the other.

Trace hadn't told her about his ownership of the family ranch or his purchase of the rodeo stock business. Or his intention to quit his job at Whistle Rock and return home. He hoped she'd agree to come with him.

If not? Well...he wouldn't allow himself to consider her not moving north.

Touching her number, he waited through three rings before she answered. "Hey."

"Hey, yourself."

He shifted the phone to his other hand. "Is this a good time to talk?"

"Great. I'm on a break. What's going on?"

"Dad is home and doing fine."

"That's great news, Trace. How's Audrey doing?"

"Relieved to have him home. I expect her to crash from exhaustion soon. Once I know my parents are all right, Koa and I will drive back. There's a lot we have to talk about."

"Yes, I know." She glanced over her shoulder to see Nacho walking toward her, waving an envelope.

"How are you doing?"

"Busy. I miss Koa, and you." Taking the envelope from Nacho, she mimed a thank you. It was from the state and held her birth certificate. Tearing it open, she scanned the documents. "Oh my..." Her voice trailed off.

"What is it, Em?"

She glanced around, eyes wild with emotion. "I need to call you back."

"Is everything all right?"

"Um...I'm not sure. I have to go." She ended the call before Trace could say anything more.

Running to the barn, she found it empty. Emma knew Virgil, Jasper, Monica, and Lily had left early for the airport. A good number of ranch employees, including her, and several guests had gotten up early to send them off.

Forcing herself to slow down and think, she leaned against an empty stall, checking the birth certificate once more. She hadn't misread it.

Emma knew she should call Trace. Pulling out her phone, she called him. He picked up right away.

"Are you all right, Em?"

"I...um...I..."

"Emma, take a breath and calm down."

She did as he suggested, breathing in and out several times before speaking. "I think my real father is working at the ranch."

He said nothing for several seconds. "At Whistle Rock?"

"Yes. You haven't met him. His name is Rance Nelson, he's an ex-rodeo cowboy, and is about the same age as Jasper. Wyatt hired him on earlier this week."

"All right. Why do you believe he's your father?"

"Hold on. I'm sending you a picture. Okay, it's off. You should have it soon."

"Got it." A moment passed before he whistled. "If this information is correct, looks like you're right. Nelson is listed as your father."

"What do you mean about the information being correct?"

"I'm being cautious, Em."

"Do you think my mother lied on the form?"

"You know her better than me. After everything we've learned the last couple weeks, what do you think?"

"I should talk to her before approaching Rance."

"That's a good decision. Talk to Pauline, then call me. If you want, I can come down within a couple days."

"You'd do that?"

"Don't you understand I'd do anything for you, Emma?"

"I wasn't sure."

"Well, I would. I'd hope to drive down in three days, so it's not a problem to return the day after tomorrow. Making sure Mom is set to take care of Dad's recovery is important to me."

"Of course it is. Let me call Mother. Then we can decide what to do next. Trace?"

"Yeah?"

"Thank you."

"Pauline was always a mystery to me, son. She always seemed to have her secrets." Audrey prepared a plate of food for Cooper, omitting butter, gravy, and dessert from his dinner. "Still, I'm surprised she never told Emma about her real father. From my point of view, that wasn't right."

Setting the last of the dinner dishes in the washer, he leaned against the kitchen counter. "I'm not sure Em will ever fully trust Pauline again."

"Understandable. It's a crime the way Pauline manipulated the two of you. Do you think Rance Nelson is her father?"

"That's what the birth certificate says. She's going to talk with Pauline."

Audrey's mouth twisted into a grimace. "I'll pray the woman answers Emma with the truth."

They both quieted when Trace's phone rang. Grabbing it from the counter, he saw Emma's face. "Yeah, babe."

"It's him, Trace."

"Pauline confirmed it?"

"Yes. I'm trying to decide what to do."

"Wait for us to get back to Whistle Rock. I spoke with Mom. She's certain Dad is doing fine. She thinks we should drive down tomorrow. We can figure it out when I get there."

"It's hard not to say something."

"I know, sweetheart. After this many years, one more day isn't going to make a difference."

"You're right. Are you really driving down tomorrow?"

"Yep. Me and Koa. A good friend is following us down. You remember Jake Kelman?"

"Your best friend. Does he want to work here?"

"I'll explain everything tomorrow. Love you."

"Love you too, Trace."

Emma hung up, feeling exhausted. Not from work, but the emotional stress of learning Rance Nelson was indeed her father.

Her mother hadn't wanted to confirm what was on the birth certificate. After sustained prodding from Emma, she'd relented, admitting the certificate was accurate.

Then she'd dug in her heels, refusing to answer any other questions about the man. No matter how Emma asked, then pleaded, Pauline ignored her daughter. They'd hung up with the same chasm between them. A breach Emma feared might never close.

Firing up her laptop, Emma began the search she'd put off until now. Starting by typing in Rance's name, the number of hits surprised her.

Most of the articles focused on his rodeo career. He'd competed in team roping and steer wrestling, making it to the National Finals Rodeo several times. There were pictures of him wearing championship buckles, with beautiful women on either side. He always had a broad smile and expressive eyes.

There were a few other articles of him at charity events. Most were for children's causes. A few for fallen rodeo competitors, and others for first responders. None of the articles mentioned a wife or family, which made her wonder if he'd ever remarried.

It took two hours to read all the articles and copy them to files on the laptop. Emma made notes while scanning the various commentaries. What surprised her was his involvement in the Fellowship of Christian Cowboys.

"Who are you, really?" Emma asked herself while shutting down the computer.

Slipping under the covers, questions about Rance Nelson played across her mind. With all the research, she still had a long list of questions for him. A man, her father, who was still a mystery.

Chapter Twenty-Eight

Emma couldn't stop the internal jitters as she waited for Koa and Trace to arrive. She'd expected them soon after lunch. At three o'clock, they still hadn't arrived. She stifled the urge to call. No one liked to be nagged, so Emma decided to wait another hour before pulling out her phone.

She'd spotted Rance several times since breakfast. It had taken all her self-control to stop herself from confronting him, ask why he'd walked out on her and his wife. But Emma had promised Trace they'd face him together. With Rance working and living on the ranch, they had plenty of time. Then why did she feel so anxious?

Doing all the dinner prep possible, she hung up her apron and headed outside. The day had turned glorious after an unusually chilly morning. The sweater in her hand wasn't needed, yet she gripped it like a lifeline.

Rance stood in the barn with Wyatt and his wife, Daisy. He hadn't noticed Emma, so she backed out far enough to watch him without him seeing her. It was his mannerisms which struck her first. They were so similar to her own.

Emma and Pauline had little in common. Their features and coloring were different, the same as their way of thinking. Emma's straight, golden brown hair and brown eyes were almost an exact match to Rance's. Although his height, at around six foot tall, was the opposite of her five-foot-three, they were both slender. Her mother carried more weight, and taming her frizzy strawberry blonde hair was always a chore.

The sound of a vehicle approaching had her turning to see Trace's truck. Rushing toward the parking area, she stopped when Koa jumped to the ground and ran to her. His firm hug warmed her heart.

"I'm hungry, Mom. Can I see if there's something in the kitchen?"

"Sure, honey."

When he took off, she faced Trace, who seemed to stalk toward her. Without hesitating, they wrapped their arms around each other, Emma lifting her face for his kiss. Pulling away, she took a step back.

"Missed you, Em."

It was exactly what she needed to hear. "I missed you too."

Jake joined them, dropping his duffle before hugging Emma. "It's been a long time."

"Too long. It's so good to see you." She looked at Trace, eager to have the talk he mentioned, and to figure out how to approach her father.

"I know you two have stuff to talk about. Why don't I take a look around?"

"First, I want to introduce you to Wyatt and Virgil. I'll let them know you're looking for work. Give Jake and me a few minutes and I'll find you so we can talk."

"I'll be in the kitchen helping Nacho get dinner ready."

Brushing a kiss across her cheek, he took off with Jake. They found Virgil talking to a group of guests by a corral. A tall, lanky man with the look of a cowboy stood next to him. Trace knew right away the man's identity. By the time he and Jake reached them, the man and guests had dispersed for their chosen activities.

"Hey, Trace. You're back. How's your father?"

"Much better, Virgil. He's back at home, and Mom is fussing over him. My guess is he'll be on his feet in a couple days. This is Jake Kelman, the man I mentioned a few weeks ago."

Virgil shook Jake's outstretched hand. "Good to meet you. We expected you a little sooner."

"I got held up at my last job."

"Are you still interested in working here?"

"Sure am."

"Great. Let me show you around." Virgil turned toward Trace. "I need to talk to you. Where are you going to be?"

"I need to speak with Emma, then I'll find you."

Nodding, Virgil walked toward the barn with Jake beside him.

Emma and Trace walked toward a stand of trees. A bench had been placed next to one, making it the perfect place to talk. They sat down, neither speaking for several minutes as their gazes settled on the mountains across the valley. Taking her hand in his, he leaned back, stretching out his long legs.

"Do you want to go first, Em?"

"I'd rather you start. How's Coop?"

"At home and doing well. Mom's hovering, as you'd expect." He hesitated, formulating what he wanted to say next. Squeezing her hand, he continued. "You know how Dad had always said the ranch would someday be mine?"

"Yes, I remember."

"He decided to turn it over earlier than anticipated."

"Because of his health?"

"Partly. Most of it has to do with being free to travel. Similar to Anson and Margie Bonner. The ranch has been mine for a while. Ever since I left the circuit."

Emma was quiet for so long he wondered if she would respond. "This means you'll need to quit your job here to run the ranch."

"True, but I don't want to go unless you and Koa are with me. I want you to marry me, Emma. Be a family again."

"Marry you..."

His heart began to pound at her lack of enthusiasm. "I love you. Being apart has been difficult on me, and I believe it has been hard on you."

"What about my job? Nacho is depending on me to take over when he retires."

"I know how much you love your job, and there may be a solution. Robber Folton put his rodeo stock company up for sale. I bought it."

Her brows lifted. "You bought it?"

"Yep."

"It must've been expensive. How could you afford it?"

"After the divorce, I channeled my anger into winning every event I entered. That was impossible, but finishing in the money happened more often than not. My record earned the interest of sponsors, who paid me even more than my rodeo winnings. Traveling expenses were minimal, and I saved every penny possible."

"That's when you started sending the extra money for Koa." She leaned closer, brushing a kiss across his cheek.

"And for you. I began mailing checks sometime during the third year. In hindsight, I should've just started a savings account."

"Mother will pay us back or she'll never see Koa again."

"You threatened her?"

"I didn't see it as a threat. More similar to the consequences of her stealing the money." Emma explained how Pauline spent the money. "If she has to sell her car, well..." She shrugged.

"You're quite the negotiator. Did she go for it?"

"Mother doesn't really have a choice if she wants to see her grandson again. Do you think I'm cruel?"

Trace shook his head. "Not at all. She's manipulated you, lied about your father, and stolen money. Repaying what she stole is reasonable, Em."

As she thought about his response, her gaze moved from him to the mountains across the valley. "All right. Now, back to my job. You said you might have a solution."

"It has to do with Folton's."

"The rodeo stock company?"

"It was for sale."

She already understood where he was going. "You made an offer."

Nodding, he rubbed his thumb over her palm. "Robber Folton accepted my offer, and the deal should close no later than early next week. It's about twenty minutes from the ranch. There will be at least ten employees. I know that's not as many as here at Whistle Rock, but you'd be in charge of their lunches. They're on their own for breakfast and dinner."

The corners of her mouth twitched, hearing the slight tremble in his voice. "I see."

"Robber's been living in the house. The kitchen is large, though the entire building can't be more than twelve hundred square feet. There are two bedrooms, one bath, and a decent sized laundry room. One of the bedrooms is used as an office. I've already hired a couple to handle the rodeo stock transactions, including contracts. Cody and Penny have a son about Koa's age. They'll be taking their lunches there, also."

She moved her other hand to rest on his arm. "I'm sure it will all be fine, Trace. My concern is my commitment to take over from Nacho. I'd be more comfortable finding a replacement before we leave."

It took a moment for him to understand the deeper meaning of her words. "Are you saying you'll marry me...again?"

A slow smile appeared on her face before she kissed him. "I believe I am."

Wyatt and Virgil listened without interrupting as Trace repeated much of what he'd told Emma. The difference was in this case, he recommended Jake as an excellent replacement for him. It didn't take too much persuading.

Both men had spent time with Jake, learning about his experience and character. He'd been open about his reason for not getting to Whistle Rock Ranch sooner, which both men understood. Compassion was an ability they respected.

"To be honest, Jake is more qualified, as he worked at a dude ranch while in high school. He's a great people person. I've seen him angry twice in all the years I've known him. I won't share the circumstances. They're private, but most people would've been enraged at both situations."

"Can you stick around a few days to acclimate him to what you've been doing?" Wyatt asked.

"Absolutely."

Virgil leaned forward. "Does he have a family we'll need to accommodate?"

"No family. He'll be fine taking my place in the bunkhouse."

"All right. We should talk about Emma leaving." Wyatt glanced at her. "I'm glad you and Trace are getting back together. I'm also sorry to see you go. Does Nacho know?"

She shook her head. "We wanted to talk to you first."

"I appreciate that. We should talk about finding your replacement."

Virgil drummed his fingers on the table next to him. "I may have an idea."

Wyatt lifted a brow. "Do I know her?"

"Doubt it. I met her at U of W. After getting her bachelor's degree in human nutrition, she was accepted at Central Wyoming University in Jackson to get her culinary science degree. The last couple years, she's worked for one of the top restaurants in Jackson. I'm almost certain she'd have an interest in Emma's job."

Wyatt's eyes and mouth twisted in confusion. "Why would she give up a job at a top restaurant to work on a ranch?"

"To be closer to home. She's from Brilliance, was a couple years ahead of us in school. Her father passed a few years ago. Her mother can no longer work more than one job, and both brothers have left the area." A look of disgust swept over Virgil's face before he concealed it.

"What about living on the ranch?"

Virgil understood Wyatt's question. "She and her brothers grew up in a tiny house, with a quadriplegic father and mother who worked two to three jobs. It was tough going. She grew from it, earned an academic scholarship to U of W. The apartment would be fine with her."

"When can you get her here to meet with us? I'm including you in this, Emma."

"I'd hoped you would let me interview a replacement, Wyatt."

"Nacho and you. Virgil?"

"I'll call her now. Excuse me." Punching in her number as he left the room, he returned a few minutes later. "She'll be here tomorrow morning."

Wyatt tapped it into his phone. "Great. What's her name?"

"Beth Jenner. Everyone's going to love her."

Chapter Twenty-Nine

"Are you ready, sweetheart?" Trace had an arm slung over Emma's shoulders, feeling her stiffen at the task before them.

"He's alone in the barn. There won't be a better opportunity."

"All right. Let's get this done." Taking her hand, they walked into the barn.

Rance Nelson stood inside the last stall, checking the hooves of a mare the Bonners had purchased a few weeks earlier. Lifting the right front leg, he used a pick to clean it out. When finished, he carefully set the hoof down, all the while talking to the mare in a soothing voice.

They watched as he continued to sooth the mare with his calm voice and comforting strokes of his hand. The man had been born to work with horses.

Trace cleared his throat, getting Rance's attention. Turning from the horse, he gave a nod before exiting the stall.

"Trace. Emma. Can I help you with something?"

Heart pounding so hard her chest hurt, Emma let go of Trace's hand. "You already know who I am. Don't you?"

Leaning against the stall, Rance slid the hoof pick into a pocket, showing no discomfort at the question. "You're my daughter."

"Why haven't you said anything?"

"You weren't ready." He glanced up as Jimmy and Owen walked into the barn. "This isn't a good place to talk."

"Let's go to Emma's apartment." Gripping her hand, Trace led the way toward the main lodge. Once inside, she motioned toward the chairs.

"Would anyone like coffee or water?"

"Water would be great," Rance replied.

"Same here," Trace said.

Removing three bottles from her small refrigerator, she handed them out before sitting down. "I want to know what happened. Why did you leave?"

Swallowing half the water, Rance capped the bottle. "You'd think the answer would be simple. It's not."

Emma shifted in her chair, setting the bottle down. "How old was I when you left?"

"Two." A small grin appeared. "You were the most gorgeous little girl I ever saw. You've turned into a beautiful woman. Driving away was the hardest thing I've ever done."

"Then why did you leave?"

"You were too young to remember the arguments between me and Pauline. They weren't occasional. We fought every day over small and big issues. The biggest being money. Pauline didn't want to work, which I understood with you being so small. The problem was she spent everything we had. There were months we had no money for food the last week of the month. When I opened a checking account without her, she went nuts. Started hitting me and calling me names even the guys on the circuit don't use." Rance looked at Trace.

"I'm sure you know what I mean. Anyway, I'd cash a check each week, giving her the money needed to buy food and other essentials. If she ran out, I'd buy what we needed. Usually food, toothpaste…stuff like that. She hated the restrictions I put on her, told everyone she was being abused. No one paid attention to her griping. They already knew about her buying whatever she wanted without limits. It wasn't hard. Pauline was the type to flaunt her purchases."

"What about other expenses?" Trace asked.

"There wasn't much other than gasoline, event registration fees, and hook-up fees for the trailer. I took care of those. Sponsor money was deposited in a savings account she couldn't access. After a while, I had that money sent to a financial planner. She was a former barrel racer who'd gotten her degree, left the rodeo, and started her own firm. She did a real good job managing my money. I planned to use it for additional expenses when you went to school. At the time, I didn't know I'd be leaving well before you started kindergarten."

"What about the arguments?"

"They continued, Emma. About money, her accusing me of cheating." He held her gaze. "Which I never did. We weren't sleeping together, so I'd bed down in my truck or a buddy's trailer. There were days I never saw her. That meant I wouldn't see you, either. It was a miserable time."

Emma let this information settle in before raising the other issue, which baffled her. "Mother says you never contacted her again or sent any money. She insists you packed your truck and drove off without letting her know you wouldn't be back."

Scrubbing a hand down his face, Rance gave an almost imperceptible shake of his head. "Your mother always had a knack for presenting issues to her advantage. Pauline knew I was leaving. We discussed it several times, along with her desire to divorce. She refused to travel to rodeos any longer. Knowing she'd have to work if we divorced, I set her up with a friend of mine who was willing to watch you when Pauline was gone. I also helped her find work." Rising, he grabbed another bottle of water and sat back down. His jaw tightened, then relaxed.

"Regarding money, I sent her a check every month until you turned nineteen. I have the cancelled checks to prove it. Money's always been an issue with her. She craves it the same as air and water. Pauline never trusted banks. She preferred cashing the checks instead of putting them in an account. If you look hard enough, I'll guarantee she has a stash of money at her house."

Emma's throat constricted, preventing her from forming a response. Everything her father said contradicted all she believed to be true. Her mother altered the truth to suit her purposes. It made Emma sick to realize how she'd been lied to all these years.

Trace recognized the anguish on her face, reaching out to take her hand. "This is a lot to take in, Rance."

"I realize it is. If you confront Pauline, she'll deny it all. That's why I'm offering to show you the cashed checks. The woman who babysat Emma years ago has offered to speak with you about what she knows. I'll give you her contact information if you want to talk to her."

"I don't need to see anything, Father. I've suspected some of what you've shared for a long time." She explained how Pauline had kept Trace's checks for herself. "I'm not sure what we'll do if she refuses to pay it back."

"File in small claims court. Even the thought of her having to answer for stealing might be enough to spark Pauline into making payments."

"Unfortunately, the amount owed is much more than the small claims limit," Trace answered. "I'm leaning toward Emma's idea of not allowing Pauline to see Koa until the money is repaid."

Rance nodded. "It's sad you must resort to keeping her grandson away. What you must remember is she brought it on herself. You can forgive her behavior, and pray she'll change. The funds earmarked for Koa's education are different. It's similar to someone stealing donations from the church till. Forgive, pray, but hold the person accountable."

Emma nodded. "You're right. I don't want to lose touch with her over money. But she does need to change her ways."

"What else do you want to know?" Rance directed the question to both of them.

Licking her lips, Emma asked what had been weighing on her. "Was coming to Whistle Rock Ranch intentional?"

He smiled. "Intentional. I've followed Trace's career since the two of you married. When I heard Trace retired and took a job here, I figured you'd be close by. It's time I got to know my daughter, and my grandson."

Warmth spread through Emma at the honesty in his features. "Way past time."

"You know Emma and I are divorced?" Trace asked.

Rance met his expectant gaze. "Yes. My question is, for how much longer?"

Trace shot a look at Emma. "If I have my way, not much longer. We just agreed to remarry."

"Is that a fact? Well, I might be able to help you."

Eyes narrowing, Trace reached out to take Emma's hand. "How so?"

"It's good news. I'm an ordained minister."

Wyatt shook Trace's hand before giving Emma a quick hug. "That's great news. I hope you'll consider having the ceremony at the ranch."

"We hadn't talked about where we'd marry. We do have a minister," Trace said.

"Who's that?"

"Rance Nelson. He's an ordained minister."

"I'll be darn. Another reason for you to have the ceremony here. Not to mention our great food. If you're worried about your parents, Trace, I can send someone to drive them down. They're welcome to stay in one of the cabins. Do you have any idea of a date?"

The whole marriage discussion was moving way too fast for Emma. "We haven't talked about it. I'd rather have the ceremony sooner rather than later. Trace?"

The smile lit up his face. "Fine by me."

"How about Saturday, the week after next? There are very few guests that week. Do you mind if they want to watch?"

"Not at all, Wyatt. Does this sound all right to you, Em?"

"So, it would be two weeks away?" She thought of what needed to be accomplished before then.

Wyatt checked the calendar again. "Two weeks from this Saturday."

"Okay. I'll talk to Nacho about food. Trace and I will pay for it, of course."

"Not a chance," Wyatt said. "You tell him what you want. We'll take care of the rest. And prepare yourself. Daisy and Lily will want to help you select a dress. My mother may also want to be involved."

Her head began to spin. She hadn't expected accepting Trace's marriage proposal to trigger such rapid actions. They all turned at the soft knock on the door.

"Come on in," Wyatt called.

The door opened slowly, Koa peeking in. When he saw his parents, he marched forward, his serious gaze moving between the two.

"Are you guys getting married?"

"Where did you hear that, son?" Trace asked.

"From Grandpa Rance. So, are you?"

They didn't even ask how he found out Rance was his grandfather.

Threading his fingers through Emma's, Trace gave a slow nod. "Yes, we are."

The brightest smile they'd ever seen broke out across Koa's face as he thrust his fist into the air.

"Yes!"

Epilogue

The two weeks flew by. Wyatt had been right. Daisy and Lily appointed themselves Emma's wedding coordinators.

The three found a dress and shoes at a small boutique in Brilliance. Thanks to an application on Daisy's computer, announcements were handed out or mailed within a few days. Lydia, at Brilliance Coffee & Bakery, designed a beautiful cake, and Nacho had completed an early afternoon lunch menu.

At fifteen minutes to noon two weeks later, Trace and Emma stood in front of her father, with Koa between them. About forty friends and guests at the ranch gathered behind them to watch the ceremony.

After obtaining approval from Cooper's doctor, he and Audrey had accepted Wyatt's offer of a ride and use of a guest cabin. Audrey had taken one look around before declaring it *delightful*. Unsurprising, yet disappointing, Pauline had declined their invitation, sighting other obligations. A day later, Emma had received a cashier's check for a few thousand dollars as a first payment.

"Ladies and gentlemen, I'd like to introduce Trace and Emma Griffin." Holding hands, they walked forward as the crowd surged toward them.

Wyatt's brothers, Jonah and Gage, congratulated them, making sure Trace and Emma knew they were always welcome at the ranch. Anson and Margie repeated the invitation, as did most everyone who worked at the ranch.

Trace held up their joined hands, kissing her knuckles. "Let's go inside. I'm starving."

Laughing, she walked to the lodge, as hungry as her husband. Inside, she stopped, her jaw dropping. "Oh, my gosh."

The dining and living room area had been decorated with swaths of colorful fabric, specialized lighting, deep blue slip covers for the dining chairs, and incredible flower and candle centerpieces.

"Who did this?" Trace asked no one in particular.

"I'm guessing Margie, Daisy, and Lily. This is just their style, so beautiful and casual. I love it." She felt Trace drape an arm over her shoulders, drawing her close to kiss her temple.

"We'll make sure to thank them."

"You guys going to stand there or get some food?" Koa stared up at them, a couple of his friends nearby.

He'd been less than enthusiastic about leaving the ranch and his friends. When Trace assured him they'd visit a couple times a year, he began warming to the idea. Emma guessed Koa would make new friends up north and settle in fine.

Trace set a hand on Koa's shoulder. "I'm with you, buddy. Let's eat."

They shared a table with Jake, the new assistant cook, Beth, and Trace's parents. For Trace, it felt as if he were back home with his family and best friend.

Jake leaned toward the woman beside him. "Where are you from, Beth?"

"Here. How about you?"

"I'm from up north. I grew up with Trace."

Emma snatched surreptitious looks at the couple as they talked. Jake, the rodeo cowboy and ranch hand, and Beth, an educated and accomplished chef. Other than Emma's lack of formal education, they weren't much different from her and Trace.

It made her wonder…

Learn about upcoming books in **The Cowboys of Whistle Rock Ranch** series at shirleendavies.com.

Enjoy the Whistle Rock cowboys? Here's another series you might want to read The Macklins of Whiskey Bend.

If you want to keep current on all my preorders, new releases, and other happenings, sign up for my newsletter at http://www.shirleendavies.com/contact-me.html

A Note from Shirleen

Thank you for taking the time to read **The Cowboy's Second Chance Family!**

Leave a Review! If you enjoyed the, please consider posting a short review and telling your friends. Word of mouth is an author's best friend and much appreciated.

I care about quality, so if you find something in error, please contact me via email at shirleen@shirleendavies.com

Books by Shirleen Davies

Contemporary Western Romance Series

MacLarens of Fire Mountain

Second Summer, Book One
Hard Landing, Book Two
One More Day, Book Three
All Your Nights, Book Four
Always Love You, Book Five
Hearts Don't Lie, Book Six
No Getting Over You, Book Seven
'Til the Sun Comes Up, Book Eight
Foolish Heart, Book Nine

Macklins of Whiskey Bend

Thorn, Book One
Del, Book Two
Boone, Book Three
Kell, Book Four
Zane, Book Five
Josh, Book Six, Coming Next in the Series!

Cowboys of Whistle Rock Ranch

The Cowboy's Road Home, Book One
The Cowboy's False Start, Book Two
The Cowboy's Second Chance Family, Book Three
The Cowboy's Final Ride, Book Four, Coming Next in
the Series!

<u>Historical Western Romance Series</u>
Redemption Mountain

Redemption's Edge, Book One
Wildfire Creek, Book Two
Sunrise Ridge, Book Three
Dixie Moon, Book Four
Survivor Pass, Book Five
Promise Trail, Book Six
Deep River, Book Seven
Courage Canyon, Book Eight
Forsaken Falls, Book Nine
Solitude Gorge, Book Ten
Rogue Rapids, Book Eleven
Angel Peak, Book Twelve
Restless Wind, Book Thirteen
Storm Summit, Book Fourteen
Mystery Mesa, Book Fifteen
Thunder Valley, Book Sixteen

A Very Splendor Christmas, Holiday Novella, Book
Seventeen
Paradise Point, Book Eighteen,
Silent Sunset, Book Nineteen
Rocky Basin, Book Twenty
Captive Dawn, Book Twenty-One, Coming Next in the
Series!

MacLarens of Fire Mountain

Tougher than the Rest, Book One
Faster than the Rest, Book Two
Harder than the Rest, Book Three
Stronger than the Rest, Book Four
Deadlier than the Rest, Book Five
Wilder than the Rest, Book Six

MacLarens of Boundary Mountain

Colin's Quest, Book One,
Brodie's Gamble, Book Two
Quinn's Honor, Book Three
Sam's Legacy, Book Four
Heather's Choice, Book Five
Nate's Destiny, Book Six
Blaine's Wager, Book Seven
Fletcher's Pride, Book Eight
Bay's Desire, Book Nine
Cam's Hope, Book Ten

Romantic Suspense

Eternal Brethren, Military Romantic Suspense

Steadfast, Book One
Shattered, Book Two
Haunted, Book Three
Untamed, Book Four
Devoted, Book Five
Faithful, Book Six
Exposed, Book Seven
Undaunted, Book Eight
Resolute, Book Nine
Unspoken, Book Ten
Defiant, Book Eleven

Peregrine Bay, Romantic Suspense

Reclaiming Love, Book One
Our Kind of Love, Book Two

Find all of my books at:
https://www.shirleendavies.com/books.html